THE UPSIDE-DOWN VOICE THAT SPEAKS BACKWARDS —

Selected Stories BY R.J. Benetti

RJ BENETTI HORROR

The Upside-Down Voice That Speaks Backwards by R.J. Benetti

Edited by Tascha Schneidel and Ben Eads

Cover art by Will Cordell - @willdrawsthings

Full wrap by Ash Ericmore

Comic book illustration by Giulio Pappalardo

To my mom, Maria, my wife, Nicole, Rod Serling, Ray Bradbury, and Harlan Ellison.

This book wouldn't exist without you.

CONTENTS

INTERNATIONAL DEATH DAY

O ne day, humanity awoke, and everything changed. And I mean, absolutely *everything*. For the whole of the universe was pulled inside out, forcibly, without consent.

The meaning of life was forever confounded, forever obstructed, in ways much weirder than my words can explain.

Elders everywhere, unknowingly awaiting cardiac arrest, or knowingly suffering from a terminal illness, people leaping off buildings or slitting their wrists or sticking their heads in ovens, soldiers and gang members being shot or exploded or strangled, infants born without breath or functioning grey matter, people hit by trains or crisped by planes crashing into cliffs, heroin and crank and coke addicts overdosing; they all had one thing in common. None of them, not one of them, passed to the other side.

None of them *could*.

Something went wrong. Whether it was a glitch in the stream of numbers permeating existence, or a unilateral decision by the Gods or Goddesses, or an alien race tampering with what we thought we knew... everything was different, and it seemed it would stay that way, forever.

Beginning on the afternoon of June 31st, 2:37 p.m. EST, no one on Earth had the ability to willingly or accidentally harm themselves or die. The concept of death was now orchestrated by regularities. It kept a tight schedule, never missing an appointment.

For it fell on the same day, at the same time, every subsequent year. Like clockwork.

October 2nd at 3:53 p.m. A time of quiescence and reverence which came to be called, Death Day, internationally.

On this day, the Reaper reaped his harvest with one swoop of his scythe. A slice, as masterful as it was murderous, took millions upon millions upon millions, no other minute of the year.

No matter how much I tried, I couldn't die.

Not unless omnipotent reality allowed it.

I shot myself in the face over a hundred times; I sheathed my feet in cement, then fell forward into the Potomac River; I doused myself in gasoline and struck a match; I chain-smoked cigarettes until my throat was ornamented with tumors: I'm still here.

My uncle and a few aunts died though, and some cousins, one parent, and a few friends, when the minute hand clicked to 3:53. Spanning continent to continent, it became a holiday of sorts, a somber day of dreaded farewells. People would gather in their living rooms, watching the clock on the television, as if it were New Year's Eve.

But the atmosphere was always tense. Those that wanted or deserved to go almost never did. There seemed to be no formula on the part of the wide-sweeping murder. Autocrats were often spared whilst saints keeled sidewise. It came to the point where no one knew what was worse: immortality or a hyper-punctual extinction.

Before, when death was a certainty allotted to every one of us, it was widely considered undesirable. Now, that it might be withheld, for eternity perhaps, the desire was not one necessarily of wanting, but of confusion.

Why was this happening?

Animals still died whenever probable. But not us. Not I and not you. Not unless it was that day and not unless we were fated for expiration.

It was the International Death Day on my thirty fifth year, that I lost my will to go on.

I was sitting around my cousin's living room with pals, my girl-friend, and other living relatives. Whimpering. Everyone was in preemptive mourning, for no one knew who was to go. Could it be me? Could it be my girlfriend or my nephews or my nieces or my grandmother? Could it be my neighbor? Could it be all of my neigh-bors? Could it be everyone on the planet except for me?

That thought was my waking nightmare. Of life completely isolated. Never dying. That was why I whimpered. That was why we bid each other farewell, as many sobbed and got drunk, and everyone decried the current state of affairs.

On that day, a decade removed from the first Death Day, seventy-five percent of the earth's population suffered coronary thrombosis. Everyone in the house, except for me and my cousin Benny, took their last breath. Some toppled forward. Some slumped over. Some clutched at their chests. Some smiled as they held hands. My girl-friend was smiling. And I was crying. Because she was gone. I told Benny to beat me in the head with a fireplace poker. He did. And I was fine, physically.

It was a nightmare. I remember holding her, she'd gone limp in my arms. And I remember looking around the room, my grandma had fallen through her glass coffee table. My nieces were curled on the ground like sleeping pups. My best friend sat still and breathless as beer poured onto his jeans and soaked the sofa cushion beneath him.

Only Benny and I remained. Fucking Benny.

RESOURCES WERE EVERYWHERE, there was an abundance of jobs, and an abundance of confusion. On the following Death Days, all one-hundred and forty-seven of them (I continued aging, but my heart kept beating somehow), it seemed like less and less people were dying. As I said earlier, I tried every which way to end it, but it seemed my life wasn't mine to take. And, as an ancient, desiccated fig-of-a-human, my worst nightmare came to pass.

I found myself without company... Benny died in mid-sentence one year—he just slowed his speech and stopped blathering about whatever the fuck he was blathering about. I shook him. Gently.

"Benny, wake up... Benny? You asshole... Benny?"

He left me alone.

I'd grown to hate him. Don't get me wrong, he was my only companion for decades upon decades, but still, I'd miss him. I tried to remember his stupid sayings and his odd, disordered thoughts oozing from his narrow face.

Companionship was over.

But not life.

When my story should have ended, the book would not shut. The sick author kept on scratching and scribbling nonsensical words on his parchment with his mocking quill. His inkwell, bottomless and dark.

Everyone was gone, except me. And every night I walked the streets, very slowly, since I was ancient, screaming to find another soul. Another person to commiserate with. Another person to shoulder my burdens, while I shouldered theirs.

And finally, on one gloom-obscured night as I walked the streets, a solitary voice answered me from the darkness.

It was a figure, neither man nor woman, slumping upon a milkcrate, beneath a glimmering tapestry of cobwebs. It echoed my words back to me when I yelled. Delighted, I shuffled slowly to the figure and as I drew nearer, I saw who it was: The Grim Reaper, pondering life and death, his skeletal hands propping up his skull.

"Hi..." I said nervously.

"Hi," he repeated back.

"W-why, why," I stammered, "am I still here, when everyone else has gone away?"

"Revelations 9:6."

"What??"

"And in those days, shall men seek death, and shall not find it; and shall desire to die, and death shall flee from them," the Grim Reaper said.

"This is all from the Bible?"

"No. Hm. Book's an imaginary thing. Even so, a broken clock is right twice a day, or however that saying goes. What I mean is, the verse seems applicable to you."

"So, you don't know what's going on? You don't know why I'm the only one still here!? You're the Grim Reaper for Christ sakes!"

"Listen, relax, calm down. I'm not sure, exactly. I was laid off over a century ago. Said I was too random. Too sloppy."

"What!?"

"Yeah. Some young kid took my position and streamlined the whole thing. Must've forgot about you. Lost your name in a filing cabinet or something."

"But why are you here?"

"Don't know. I've nowhere else to go. With everyone else gone, I guess I was forgotten, too."

THE MAN IN THE PURPLE HAT

I saw him again today. He was in the library. Watching me. With his dull-grey eyes unblinking. And his old and weathered white face barely looking like a human's.

He wears a purple baseball cap. Always, whenever I see him... which is often. He is wearing that logo-less, purple, bent-brimmed, baseball cap.

I don't know what he wants with me. When I saw him today, standing oddly beside the children's fiction section, he seemed almost surprised that I had noticed him.

But I always do.

The man in the purple hat might not be human. There's something missing in him. Like he's some deviously leering mannequin made flesh, or a facsimile of a real person. He just stares every time, like his shadow is being cast into our world, from some horrid and unearthly realm.

I put my books down, and I leave. I don't even bother to check them out. I leave and I don't look over my shoulder. I know he is watching me.

Like I said, this happens a lot.

In the beginning, I explained it away by mere coincidence. And yet. The way he makes my skin crawl. No. There's something wrong with him. I know it. I can feel it in my bones.

The next day I'm walking, just walking, in my boring little

Arkansas town. I'm holding my purse to my side so it doesn't swing. And I see him. The brim of his purple hat is poking out behind some tall hedges. And then, the rest of his pallid face. Eyes widened. Staring. Boring a hole into me.

I stop. My body chills in an instant. I can't believe it. I feel like I can't swallow. What does he want? I keep walking, quickening my pace towards my stalker, and he runs, suddenly, and clambers over a fence.

I can barely catch my breath. I don't get it.

A week passes. I see his purple hat in crowds. I see his strange, gangly build in almost every bus stop. And I see him glaring at me in my local shopping mall.

The man in the purple hat is curled over the banister on the upper floor. I felt his eyes before I even saw him. He's looking down at me like some vulture. His face is crisscrossed with wrinkles. Grey hairs poke from the sides of his sweat-soaked hat.

I move as fast as I can. I look up. And there he is. Tracing my every step. Following me on the floor above. I sprint to my car, sobbing. I speed away, ignoring stop signs and signals.

IT'S GETTING REALLY hard to sleep at night. I wake up trembling, screaming. There's a figure leering in the corner of the dark room. When I switch on the lights, there's no one there.

Yet, I can still feel his eyes on me. Warm. Repulsive. Wanting.

It happened in the shower, too. I was exfoliating my skin with my pink gloves. Steam rose in whorls. Soap suds turned the flowing water into a burbling froth.

I dipped my head beneath the showerhead, feeling the stream of warm water clearing the soap from my eyes. And there he was.

There. In the periphery. Behind the shower curtain. The purpleness of his hat was enough to make me choke. His figure. I saw it too. A lumbering, prowling monster.

I screamed bloody murder. It was all I could do. Then I lost my footing, slamming into the tile wall... only to wake hours later. The shower had been shut off, but the showerhead *drip, drip, dripped* on my exposed thigh. Like a pervert's touch. I was nude, and I saw a small bruise above my wrist.

The curtain, I noticed, had been drawn back. So the man in the purple hat could watch. Could peep. But there was nobody there. He was gone. And I sobbed.

THAT WEEKEND, our small town had its annual carnival. There would be a Ferris wheel, cotton candy, tilt-a-whirls, mirror mazes and laughter aplenty. I didn't want to go. I felt I needed to stay in. Barricaded in my room with every kitchen knife I could find. But my friend Stacy convinced me otherwise.

"C'mon, get out and get some fresh air for a while. It will do you some good," she said.

So, I ended up going. I was trembling the entire time. And I usually love the carnival. But everything had the lurid tint of purple. The balloons. The ring toss game. Even the stuffed animals. To say I was on edge would be the understatement of the century. I could feel him watching me.

Crowds converged, and I tiptoed, a scared little girl caught in the middle of happy-go-lucky mayhem. Stacy grabbed my arm. Tried to calm my nerves.

"Isn't this gangbusters?" she said.

I tried to smile. But only gritted my teeth.

The crowds thickened around us while we strode. Congealed, as the confluence of bodies interchanged in a trillion and one figures.

Then I saw him. I was staring at his back, but I knew it was him. The man in the purple hat.

I broke Stacy's hold and grabbed him by his thin shoulder. He reeled and glared with his lurid, white face.

"WHY ARE YOU FOLLOWING ME!?" I screamed.

Suddenly, he attacked me. Knocked me to the ground, cursing hysterically. Kicked and punched me as my skull bounced upon the asphalt. The crowds wrested him off.

I could see him wheezing. Mad. Flustered.

"This person's been following me for weeks. I can't escape her! She torments me. Breaks into my home. You have to believe me! She's a monster! Arrest her!" cried the man in the purple hat.

Soon, a group of security guards apprehended me. And I swear I saw him smile.

FREAKSHOW

There was a strong scent of trash festering under an abnormally hot sun—along with the sweet stink of funnel cakes, sunbaked horse skeletons, pretzels, Mexican street corn, and greasily fried turkey thighs.

And that's not to mention the odor of the sweating men and women milling about in the arid, beige terrain that spread out for miles and miles.

The place was located in the southwestern part of the Great Basin of Nevada, which is concave like a large and very dry sink, filled with dirt.

The borders of the Basin commingled with the Mojave Desert—and if one peered squinty-eyed into the distance, they'd see it occupied by geologically ravishing anomalies, like orange buttes and cragged pinnacles. They'd also see some cacti, brush and sediment leading to an indistinct horizon washed in a radiating, neon-green light.

And if one hearkened on this particular evening, they could hear the chortle-din of laughter from the happy-go-lucky customers munching down their bags of candy corn, guzzling fizzy-pop or frothy beers.

The noises infused the lively scene, which was inhabited by red and white candy-cane-banded tarpaulins sagging like loose skin on sharp breasts pointed towards the red-orange sky. The carnival tents were the emblem of the freakshow. They were an indicator, or a tell-tale sign bespeaking its presence.

When one saw those red and white tents in the middle of an otherwise forsaken, almost-Martian-esque landscape, one knew they were in for a treat. It was evident that the humdrum routine of everyday life was primed for some interruption—by the traveling freakshow.

Thus, it became overrun with scores of curious townies and desert-dwellers, all coming to see the itinerant oddities.

And that's what brought the McGinty family there. The father, Morris, stood with his neatly parted black hair, his dumb, black-rimmed spectacles, his tucked-in button-up shirt, his creased grey trousers, and the stopwatch, tucked away in his shirt's front pocket, ticking in the same boring cadence that he spoke in.

The mother, Cordelia, had a classic 1960s style beehive hairdo, with the blonde bangs and the sides that curled out and up above her frumpy ankle-length baby blue and white dress tied around the waist.

And the little boy, Calvin, was as plain and unassuming as a penny—with his blue, green, and white striped shirt and his crummy jeans and his brown hair combed by his mother but now frazzled from rambunctiousness.

And his sister, Jennifer. She was the picture of normalcy, with her long brown hair with the bow on top, and her church shoes and her button nose.

They all waited in one of the many tents, peering expectantly over to the other side of a red-velvet rope—so different, that it might've been another world.

Jennifer hung on her dad's arm, making little impatient whimpers as the boy, Calvin, kicked rocks and his mother swatted him on the back of the head, ordering him to "Stop that right now! Calvin James!"

"Well... when they gunna come!" whined Calvin.

"They'll come when they're ready for the show. Just hold your danged horses, Cal, or I'll give you a whoopin' when we get home."

Finally, there was some commotion from outside the tent—the rustle of a herd, or a troupe, of people. Were they the freaks? Jennifer squeezed her dad's hand. The tent flapped open.

In walked a five-foot-five, hairless, *thing*. The McGinty family marveled. It was a strongman, and he was composed entirely of bulging muscles.

He grunted somberly while he labored to walk, for his legs were encumbered by extra calves and extra thighs that rippled up to his freakishly strong, and equally uncomfortable glutes.

His arms were jumbled mounds of biceps, forearm muscles, and deltoids, and his nearly exploding pectoral muscles twitched from the constant surge of testosterone.

His little bald head, which was nearly engulfed in his trapezius muscles, poked out and peered angrily like a roseate hemorrhoid.

Although the bald man was mightily strong, it was clear that he was handicapped by his awkward musculature. He grunted and imploringly studied the smirking family with his beady eyes that bulged from his head.

Calvin giggled.

Next entered a woman wearing an all-black pioneer dress, which matched her very, *very*, jet-black beard. The wiry face hair was shaped like a corrugated spade that crimped out over the buttons on the skirt's rounded neckline.

Little Jennifer drew her gaze from the bottom of the frilly dress all the way up to the gathered sleeves and the five-button cuffs and over the pocket holding a yellow hankie to the woman's barbarous face.

She had an almost puritanical look to her—as if Stonewall Jackson had had gender-reassignment surgery.

Calvin squealed and his father, Morris, clutched his shoulder in an effort to silence him. Three sisters had entered the tent. They were conjoined by the sides of their torsos and they moved in a weird, cumbrous way, like their feet were in constant discord with one another and each one of their toes had a different idea of where it wanted to trot. The Siamese triplets ogled the family, crossing their eyes in every direction. Cordelia bowed at them, in a welcoming sort of way.

In addition to being conjoined, the triplets were microcephalic. Each one of their respective heads was the size of a modest nectarine.

In P.T. Barnum's days, they would've been called pinheads, but that wasn't acceptable in the present here and now. The triplets had their names stitched onto the three chests of their extra-wide skirt saying: *Beep, Bop*, and *Boop.*

The McGintys smiled at them.

A man illustrated from head to toe with whirling tattoos entered under the now crowding tent. His tongue was forked like a snake's and his pupils were horizontal dashes like those of a goat's.

He was almost completely black from all the ink and it seemed he had never cut his fingernails, for they extended from his three-fingered hands like long yellow vines—ridged with the keratinous strata of time. He also had three toes on each foot, and a pair of very sharp griffin-like talons protruding from his heels.

The inked-up-mutant hissed at the family, muttering something in a strange, forgotten language that sounded both ancient and new. Whatever he said, was unmistakably a slur.

Then, a morbidly obese man with a snakeskin koala (a koala whose skin was that of a snake's) perched on his shoulder, entered the tent on a tricycle.

It was fantastic how he rode the tricycle as it almost completely disappeared under his many folds of fat. He slowly circled 'round and 'round and eventually parked it next to the bearded lady whose eyes were piercing holes through the children.

Morris cleared his throat and touched the uppermost button of his very neat shirt.

Watching the entrance, Morris saw seven odd-shaped, thin things waddling in with their tiny feet and tiny torsos and necks that were stretched tall and long like lamp posts, going all the way up to heads that were even smaller than those of the triplets.

They were a radiating, humming neon-green, and their odd bodies were sluiced in a snot-colored slime that gathered in burbling globs in spots and dripped on the ground. Their arms were short and small, and the things shrieked as if they were frightened of the family.

Calvin nearly jumped into the air because a dog-faced boy walked into the tent next. It was possible that the boy had hereditary hypertrichosis, or werewolf syndrome, or maybe the thick brown hair that covered the entirety of his body was simply a response to his surroundings.

The hound-child and Calvin were nearly the same height.

The dog-faced-boy approached Calvin and they blinked at each other curiously from two sides of the rope. Then, the dog-faced-boy stuck out his hand to touch Calvin, only to draw back suddenly—not of his own volition.

He was yanked back by a mustachioed-thin man who had an entire Ottoman sabre lodged horizontally in his throat. His skin stretched to hold the pointed blade and the filigreed, twisting metal hilt.

"Don't you touch them!!" the man screamed. His voice whistled around the sword in his throat. "They're freaks! Look at them! Absolutely disgusting!"

Morris smiled and sort of bowed and he nudged Cordelia and she in turn nudged the children and they all doubled over, bowing with the father. The congregation of mutants started hissing and howling and yipping in response to their strange appearance.

They commented on the family's symmetrical faces and their unblemished skin and their normally sized arms and legs.

A girl with seventeen legs, who moved about like a spider, pattered up to the red-velvet rope, and spit an unknown venom on Cordelia through the third eye on her head. Cordelia bore the insult and smiled and sort of bowed again. This was their job. They were the traveling freakshow, and they needed the money.

"Calvin, Jennifer, are you ready?" asked Morris through the side of his mouth.

The children nodded and then, just as they had practiced, started doing amateurish gymnastics, tumbling and flipping, doing somersaults and cartwheels.

Cordelia and Morris sashayed their hands back and forth and danced and wiggled their shoulders for their customers.

The strongman started nodding his bald head, which was enveloped in muscles upon muscles upon muscles. And the thin-necked-long things started shrieking like train whistles gone awry.

The bearded lady clapped, and the dog-faced-boy slipped under the rope and was noshing on Morris' ankle, but he kept dancing just the same and *Beep* and *Bop* and *Boop* started laughing wildly.

"FREAKS!! FREAKS!! FREAKS!!" the crowd shouted. The fat man threw apple cores and rib bones at them that he had stored under his folds.

His snakeskin koala chirped.

THAT NIGHT, the McGinty family and all the other families from all the other tents started packing their things away. Calvin and Jennifer fell asleep outside of their tent as it was being taken down.

Morris and Cordelia quietly strapped gas masks onto them and carried them to the back of their red and white RV, so they could sleep more soundly. Beholding their slumbering children, they smiled.

The crowds were gone and with them the insults and the hurt. But the families now had full pockets, stuffed and brimming.

All was quiet, save for a soft hum from not too far away.

And the air no longer smelled of funnel cakes... but of acrid warmth.

Although it was well past midnight, they could all work by the light of the neon-green radiation coming up from over the horizon. The Nevada nuclear test site was never brighter. And in a way, it symbolized all the nuked-out sites in the world, which were all over and everywhere.

The performers, the unmutated, the uninitiated, the freaks as they were often called, were very much in the world's minority. And being as such, they had to scrape by, any way they could.

GATHER YOUR STONES

C het "The Chainsaw" Jones, the Florida panhandle's most notorious mask-wearing serial killer, hobbled both tall and forlorn from his eight by eight-foot prison cell.

Chet was a seven by three-foot person.

Alabaster like a specter, wet like a slug, he left a box of scuffed-up steel walls and passed through a single metal entryway, which lead to anything but freedom.

The cell's general demeanor and décor made Chet feel he was in an industrial sized oven. Slowly heating and baking. His future, bearing down upon him like a fang-toothed silverback gorilla, wasn't very promising.

His arms and legs were shackled many times over in concatenated fashion, so as to control his alleged bloodthirstiness and his proclivity to tear and rend the bodies of the unfortunate "do-gooders" who got in his way.

He'd been charged, and subsequently convicted, of the spree killings of fourteen individuals living in a retirement community in a very upscale area of Pensacola, Florida.

The retirement community was called "Sol Villas." It is rumored that Telly Savalas, who is known for the police procedural series Kojack, lived there at one point in time.

The killer used a chainsaw to dismember the elderly and wore a pair of women's panties over his vile face as he heehawed and barked like a maniac. Apple crumbles would forever be un-eaten. Ensure and Arnold Palmer's would loiter un-drank.

Afterwards, Chet allegedly went to Pensacola State College and hacked up some students in a food court.

On January 24th, 1995, he was scheduled for a much anticipated execution.

And the rest, as they say, was history.

A HORDE, numbering in the thousands, had gathered outside of what'd been Chet's home for the past decade: Florida State Prison. This was to be the oddest tailgating situation of the penitentiary's tenured existence.

They waved signs like, "BURN CHET BURN," and "I HOPE YAR CHAINSAWED IN H... E... DOUBLE-HOCKEY-STICK," and "FOR ASHLEY!"

Ashley Masters was one of the six college students decapitated by Chet, the crowd believed.

The death of the serial killer, which was due to take place in no less than ten minutes, caused much merriment and celebration among the ranks of visitors to the prison's lawn.

They barbecued hotdogs and burgers and wings and guzzled booze in various forms, wearing t-shirts and sweatshirts showing the tall man strung up by his neck (although he was to be done in by the electric chair and not the noose).

Most of the images the crowd had on their shirts and posters depicted Chet as a bearded, long haired, brutish-looking fellow, with scratched-out eyes and added-on devil horns.

However, inside the prison, Chet looked much different. He was bald like a fetus—a tall one, at that—tremoring as he walked "the last mile." In spite of his very low IQ, which caused most to deem him a dim or a halfwit, he did have a sense of what was coming.

Fright iced his bones.

The shackles clanked and rattled as he shuffled forth at the impetus of four guards, with faces stoic despite the occasional sneer. The other prisoners taunted "The Chainsaw," hollering nonsense and blathering hot air.

They hooted like demented owls, scratching 'round in their respective cages, waiting for their time to come.

Chet dropped his bald head.

Outside, people were throwing up clouds of confetti and moon-walking and doing "the cabbage patch" on their cars as Jon P. Malphus, a correspondent from WBBH, the local news station, and an affiliate of NBC, made the rounds, thrusting his microphone under people's chins while his gangly cameraman trailed close behind.

The reporter, an eagle-faced biped bereft of humor, was determined to get to the bottom of the human emotion on the lawn... for the ratings.

The chatter and excitement swelled.

Malphus spotted someone in the crowd, she was just like everyone else, but singularly unique in her own way.

This was his target: a stub of a lady, with blue-lensed aviator sunglasses and a tank top that said, "ELECTROCUTE ALL SINNERS!" in runny black ink.

"How do you feel about what's going on here today?" Malphus pushed the microphone under the woman's wiry chin.

"I feel like it's about damn time we hold people responsible. I mean, just look at what we got going on in the country. Ya know?"

"How do you mean..."

"Well, all these strange languages and cultures coming in, and these disrespectful kids... I mean what that Chainsaw fella did to those elderly. You know I'm getting older misself, I think he deserves to die in hard pain, just like he made others suffer!"

"Thank you, mam. May I ask your name?"

"It's Adele. My name is Adele."

"Thank you, Adele," said Malphus. And he walked off.

The cameraman hustled in tow, shouldering the heavy equipment and sweating like a fiend in a geyser of bubbling syphilis. Malphus approached a group of twenty-somethings huddled 'round the bed of a truck; they were laughing as they guzzled warm beers.

The group focused on some shenanigans occurring in the epicenter of their fraternal circle. And as Malphus strode closer, he could see the strange and unsettling happening they entertained themselves with.

A young man was sitting in a foldable beach chair with an empty beer box on his head, miming the act of being electrocuted as the others cheered his theatrical death. He tensed his muscles and quivered.

The others rejoiced and whooped.

The beer-box-head-person began regurgitating foam, spitting it up on himself. Seeing this, Malphus gesticulated wildly, ordering his cameraman to catch everything. So, he did.

And they all laughed as their friend fell sidewise from his chair, slamming his back and shoulder on the trodden grass. Malphus grinned his perfect-for-TV-grin.

Inside the prison, the shaven Chet was entering a small-sinister room with a one-way glass wall. The room smelled stale, like it'd been a repository for desiccated moths.

Two corrections officers continued to shepherd Chet, standing abreast on opposite sides while the large man shuffled.

A hearty terror contorted the condemned man's face as he saw the wooden electric chair and all its binding gadgetry. It jutted stark and lethal from the middle of the otherwise undecorated room.

Never, in all of Chet's unfortunate life, had a piece of furniture been so menacing. His knees wobbled and the two very large, yet still much smaller men beside him kept him standing, moving forward and onward. His mouth lost its moisture; he tried to breathe, but his cheeks just suctioned to the sides of his teeth, making a soft squelching noise.

Old Sparky creaked as Chet sat down. His eyes welled with tears as he stared at the reflective wall while the guards fastened him in.

"I didn't do it..." Chet whispered.

No one responded.

Outside, Malphus was still making the rounds, thrusting his microphone every which way in an odd, newsgathering jig. He approached a group of angry old women... or at least he thought they were angry old women.

When he drew nearer, he noticed that they were, instead, college-aged sorority girls. The abject callousness of their expressions made them seem much older.

The group waved signs with Xeroxed photos of Ashley Masters and one other sorority sister allegedly murdered by the Chainsaw-wielding Chet Jones: Bernice Flowers.

The images on the signs were of hopeful cherubic faces, full of dreams for the future. They were smiling snapshots of a place in time when graduating, then going on to a bright future seemed likely.

"C'mon, c'mon," Malphus tugged the cameraman by the elbow of his shirt.

He inched eagerly towards one of the young women, a dark brunette with tortoiseshell sunglasses and a frown cemented among her wooden features. The woman's arms were crisscrossed in front of her chest.

Malphus waggled his finger to make sure his cameraman was in position.

"Can you tell us why you're here today?" Malphus asked.

"My sisters were butchered in a food court, brutally butchered, like animals, and you ask what I'm doing here?"

"I'm sorry, miss, may I ask your name?"

"No comment."

"So, you're here to make sure justice is done on behalf of your slain friends?"

"Justice?" the girl scoffed. "Justice would mean taking a chainsaw to that psychopath and watching him bleed out while he screamed in pain. If you ask me, he's getting off easy..."

"And why are you all here..."

"To celebrate and to make sure that monster gets what he deserves."

"How do you feel today? All things considered?"

"I feel mad. Just furious. And maybe, taking this man's life might end the nightmare for all of us... only if he suffers... that's all I want... that's all I really want, really, what we all want."

The sisters howled the names of Masters and Flowers, touting their signs for the camera. Revenge had mutated their young faces.

They'd somehow become angry, acrid old beings frothing with vinegar.

"Thank you," said Malphus. He quickly turned away, noticing no one else wished to speak with him.

Chet's wide wrists were tethered to the chair's armrests with black, belt-like restraints. His large, sunken chest followed. Then his ankles, on Old Sparky's legs. He began whimpering, opening and shutting his eyes while tears dripped freely downward, wetting his lap, which'd already been wetted with another liquid, near his groin.

"I didn't do these things!" Chet began hollering, flexing and struggling within his restraints. "PLEASE! PLEASE! WON'T SOMEBODY LISTEN! I'M INNOCENT!!"

The guards glared with apathy. They had put some Vaseline in their nostrils, prepping themselves for the stench of singed flesh that was sure to come in a few moments.

After the electrocution, they would need to soak their clothes in water for two to three days before washing, to fully cleanse the smell of death.

The room was heavy with oppression. Chet's fear went from his body and groped at the walls. Panicking.

The condemned saw his own reflection, gaunt and pinioned to the nefarious furnishing. He knew people were watching on the other side. Watching and waiting for the horrible death of a "terrible man."

The last thing Chet saw, before the guards strapped a brown leather mask to his face, covering all but his neck and chin, was himself, copiously sweating. Small with terror. Stewing in fear, in surprise, with eyes huge like softballs, filigreed with a smattering of burst blood vessels.

How had he gotten here? He'd been nothing more than a janitor. A simple person. A gentle one, he thought... he didn't understand the hatred in the room, or, for that matter... in the world.

Everything turned to darkness under the mask. Chet gulped for air.

Outside, Maplhus was jogging, pointing the way for the young cameraman to fully capture the growing excitement and rage. A man with a rattail punched the sky and spat upon the ground, chanting with the crowd as they counted down the minute, and the seconds therein, before Chet's death.

"Over there, look! Look! Look!"

The cameraman swiveled, capturing b-roll of some country politicians, big-stomached and snarling, spewing their condemnation. Women cheered, hugged and sobbed, as true crime enthusiasts sprinted the grounds, leaping in absolute joy. A priest waved his bible, closed his eyes and cast judgment upon Chet's soul. A Baptist minister, standing nearby beside a mud-splattered Range Rover, kept repeating the words, "let him who is without sin, cast the first stone..."

The energy was frenetic. The scorn, virally contagious. The crowd swelled, counting down, down, down, "30... 29... 28..."

Malphus was in heaven... a veritable pig in apocryphal shit. He would surely get a raise after this.

The guards placed a saline-soaked sponge on the crown of Chet's pinball head. The spring-action helmet and accompanying electrode came next: a perfect fit. They screwed the wingnut tight. They did up the chin strap, buckling it firmly with no room to wriggle. Fully ensnared, Chet whined, but his voice was muffled by the tight-drawn leather about his face.

A guard began speaking...

"Chet Mathias Jones, you are sentenced to death as a result of the conviction of multiple homicides by brutal, monstrous means. Due to your apparent guilt, as decided by Florida State's judicial system, electrocution will be used to end your life. The highest of voltages will pass through you until you are no longer among the living. No longer able to hurt honest men, women, and children. May God have mercy on your soul."

Chet moaned and sobbed in the darkness. It would be his last conscious utterance.

"Roll on two," said the guard.

Outside, the countdown neared its end... "4... 3... 2... 1..." The multitude cheered.

Secluded in his grim alcove, the executioner jammed a button on a big General Electric switchboard. The dynamo hummed to life. He then pulled a lever and currents exceeding those needed to kill a full-grown rhino began their incursion into Chet's body, causing it to knot up and spasm, jerking and rocking in the chair.

Bottles of champagne were popped, liquor was swigged, and whooping and dancing commenced on the lawn. The lights guttered nearby, within the imposing penitentiary.

They watched the execution within the darkened room, their faces set in serried rows behind the one-way glass.

Stared as boils and blisters rose from the convulsing man's corpse, while smoke tendrilled from his skull. For a full fifty-five seconds, 2,450 volts of electricity cooked Chet's insides. There was a five second intermission. Then...

"Roll on one..."

A second lever was flipped and Chet convulsed anew, wriggled as life slipped from him and into the wires, killing him for good. Ten-inch flames shot from his skull as his spirit left his body, and then, the switchboard malfunctioned.

Sparks began exploding from the controls, baking the executioner in place, causing him to collapse in an atrophied state.

Hollering, the guards turned to run, only to find no respite from the pools of blue-white electricity extending from the switchboard. Their boots landed in that which would cause an onslaught of pain.

The currents disseminated, increasing in voltage with every life claimed. Those watching the execution screamed and jostled for escape. The dark room had brightened.

It was too late.

Malphus pushed his microphone toward multiple tear-dewed tailgaters, recording their exclamations of relief.

Many said there was a special liberation in the knowledge that Chet "The Chainsaw" Jones was no longer alive.

"May his victims rest in peace, thanks for speaking with us at WBBH," said Malphus.

Neither he nor his cameraman noticed electricity streaming in a waterfall from the penitentiary's windows, barreling down its cold stone walls and onto the edge of the lawn.

Some of the partiers did, however, see the anomaly. Throng by throng, person by person, they gasped and stopped celebrating as the currents flowed toward them like a predatorial wave to an unsuspecting beach.

Sprinting, clamoring, tripping over one another, Malphus was bowled over by a firm of lawyers then trampled by a horde of unknowns.

As the crowd panicked the priest waved his bible, and the electricity overtook them all, enveloping the field and their bodies, causing them to writhe in blue-yellow pain.

Shrieks slashed the stratosphere asunder, supercharging the flickering stars in a moment of intense torment. The contorted masses jerked their limbs, and blood seeped from their now gelatinous eyes. Tongues stuck skyward and sideways.

"Let him who is without sin, cast the first stone," the Baptist preacher muttered, and strolled away, the sole of his sneaker passing the shattered lens of a TV news camera.

THE EXPERIENCER

How does one describe an Unidentified Flying Object?

Well, this one, in particular, was spherical and shapeshifting like some piece of airborne putty. It was silvery, and kind of metal-looking, like the balled-up tinfoil of an eaten sandwich, and it was dangling from a string. A *STRING*.

That's what did it, really. That's what caused the townsfolk of Cochiti Lake in New Mexico to think that their fellow denizen, Roy Santacruz, had gone insane.

You see, there are about 569 people living in the Town of Cochiti Lake on the Rio Grande.

Everybody pretty much knows everybody. And if you don't know them, you'd recognize their face at the very least.

Roy Santacruz is the local proprietor of the Pueblo De Cochiti Convenience Store. He's a mild-mannered, plump, quiet sort of guy.

You might imagine our surprise when he came bounding, in a ditheringly nervous state, through the doors of Crawford Town Hall. It was during our bimonthly community meeting no less. We were all sitting in our tired semicircle, vaguely discussing the usual topics: wares, job growth, or decline, tourism, family comings and goings and the like. Now, mind you, this takes place at nine thirty pm, so we were all pretty worn out from a day's toil.

So, this Roy Santacruz, a respected member of the community, comes barreling in. His face is all wet with sweat, eyes wild like a mad steer's. He's holding this old JVC video camcorder, thing seems vintage, from the seventies or eighties. And he's shaking it wildly in his hand saying, "I just saw a UFO! I just saw a UFO!" over and over again.

Now we were all mighty surprised, wouldn't you be? But he says he caught it on his camcorder. Was recording, fiddling with the old humdinger, pointing it at the sky when he saw this thing, this alien mothership... I'm embellishing with the word mothership, sort of a running gag in the community now.

What we saw, when he eventually showed us the footage, seemed like a cruddy, poorly formed, aluminum foil tennis ball, as I said earlier. Sort of a gray and shiny blob. It was dangling on a string, as I also previously mentioned.

We didn't know if this Roy Santacruz, a once taciturn guy, was just pulling our legs. We didn't know if he was duping us all with some mischievous teenager's idea of a practical joke. He seemed ardently serious, though. Was even quite broken up about it. Seemed to be having some sort of psychological break. A few of the wives in attendance had to calm him down. They placed towelettes on his forehead and spoke to him gentle like.

I've watched the damned video over twenty times. Looks fake to me. Whole town thinks it's a ruse. But Roy Santacruz just keeps on saying it's real. Years done passed since that strange night. Being the quack that he is, Roy has deemed himself "AN EXPERIENCER."

It's kind of spooky sounding, I reckon. He says he's Cochiti Lake's first and foremost seer of all things unidentified and flying. He now sells little trinkets, like spaceship doohickeys, and alien bobbleheads in his store.

Some conspiracy-weirdos drive three and a half hours from Roswell just to see the guy and to watch the footage. It's an alien enthusiast pilgrimage, they tell me. I imagine they're mighty let down when they see the spaceship is dangling from a damned *STRING!*

ON MARS, 33.9 million miles away, a seven-year-old Martian child is tinkering with some object. He is about three-feet tall, his head is big and bulbous, and his flesh is vermillion, just like the sprawling desert landscape he calls home. He is sitting in a big crater, working feverishly, and with complete abandon. He cranes his neck, large-yellow eyes glinting, to stare at his father who is approaching from over the crater's rim.

"What seems to be the preoccupation today, young Jibbly-Schtark?" the father asks, amused.

"I am attempting to build another one, father. A magnificent KITE to visit the earth!" the boy says.

"What happened to the last one? Burned it up on Mercury?" the father jokes.

"No, I just thought... I just felt it looked stupid. Like a balled-up piece of tinfoil or something."

"Ah, that would look rather peculiar," responds the father.

SKIN

The darkness of the corner suited Ingrit well.

Coalescing with shade and shadow, the elements of night, nobody could see her. And if no one could see her—then maybe the torment would stop.

Ingrit stared out at the surrounding room, examining everything with her little black peppercorn eyes.

These eyes were the only thing even remotely *normal* on her, and yet they seemed mere pins swallowed by the cushion of her heavily distorted face.

She had a disease.

Her skin hung about her small build like pallid curtains, with folds and wrinkles, and long swatches of unidentifiable flesh that hid her frail appendages.

If one were to shine a light in her direction, in the damp-dark corner, they would see something akin to a beige blob. Inhuman. Deformed. Lost.

But not alone.

Ingrit was tended to by her mother, Ingeborg, who regularly brought her food and drink and who helped her wash under her voluminous pleats of flesh. They lived at the outermost limits of Lanesboro, Minnesota; just the two of them.

Ingrit had always been this way, entering the world as a translucent, jellyfish-like mound. Even then, she was difficult to look at. All dodger blue and purple with coral-pink veins. A near formless newborn, just "a shape," with something vaguely human about it.

The slate-black eyes.

Ingrit's father, an abusive miner of coal, had deserted not long after her birth, thinking his wife's womb a damnable incubator for demonic entities—like his one and only daughter.

And the people in the small town, with a population less than

500, weren't much kinder than the father who left—being exceptionally cruel to the exceptionally deformed looking child.

It started soon after the birth, when haughty town women would remark on the "sad little grits" in the baby stroller.

As Ingrit grew, accumulating more and more skin, the insults rose in sharpness and pitch.

Many stores and shops refused Ingeborg's patronage—not with that meandering blob by her side—that stumbling mass with the uncomfortable glare.

People would throw things. Anything really. It became a sort of game. If you could hit Ingrit with some trash or a half-eaten meatloaf sandwich, then you were in for kudos and backslaps galore.

A man even shot at Ingrit once. Luckily, he missed. He was very drunk. And he eventually ran out of bullets.

That's when they decided to move, since the townsfolk made both Ingeborg's and Ingrit's lives a living hell.

Mother and daughter relocated to the outskirts of town; however, it didn't stop the depraved Minnesotans from hounding them, using the young girl's condition as an excuse for all of their ills.

She was a scapegoat. If anything, anything at all, went wrong, such as someone dropping a plate of scraps, then the townsfolk would say:

"It's the curse of that damned monster that lives on the hill!!!"

They regularly painted the walls of Ingeborg's new house with curses such as, "Skin-Freak!" and the "Devil's Foreskin" and "Whore Daughter."

The squat hovel made of brick began looking like a highway rest stop—all covered in graffiti and moldering with neglect—since Ingeborg had long since quit trying to clean it.

"Why do they hate me *so much*, momma?" Ingrit would say, her voice muffled by her bedspreads of skin.

"It's because you're special, Ingrit. You're different. And people are scared of what they don't understand. They don't know your heart like I do. You're the most generous and sweetest girl in the whole wide world."

"Thank you... *momma*..." a big tear rolled through the many crests and valleys on Ingrit's cheek. She blinked her dark-damp eyes... in the dark-damp corner... of her dark-damp little house.

From then on, when an insult would be flung her way, like the time a young towheaded boy called her a "human bagpipe filled with sick air," Ingrit would remind herself of her mother's words. She was just *special*.

That's why they didn't understand her.

That's why they insulted her.

That year she turned eleven.

Ingeborg never showed her daughter her reflection, in fear that she would get too upset. And Ingeborg, too, tried not to stare for too long. Even though it was difficult to avert her eyes—her daughter's skin was growing and was beginning to fill up the entire room.

She had to lift flesh folds up to find her daughter's mouth, to feed her, and soon, she had to brush away skin so she could see her tiny coal-black eyes.

Ingrit became more and more immobile, until she was confined totally, to her dark-damp little room.

THE FOLLOWING year was one of Lanesboro's hardest.

The mining industry, which had been its lifeblood and had employed most everybody there, even the women and children, was going under.

Ingeborg made ends meet by selling goat's milk and sheepskin blankets, which she sewed by hand, gnarling her knuckles. This shouldn't have mattered, but since the coal industry was floundering, many in the village began resenting that she and her misshapen Ingrit were doing just *Ok*.

It all came to a head on July 3rd, 1928, when a coal mine collapsed, killing thirteen young men and two old ones and one middle-aged woman.

The town was devastated.

Not only for the loss of life, but also because it was one of the last of the "coal-rich" mines left. They had to worry about where their food would come from in the months to follow, since their most lucrative export might be kaput.

You could feel the vexation in the air.

INGEBORG STROLLED HUMBLY INTO TOWN. With her head downcast, fixated on the grease stained laces of her balmoral boots, trying not to upset anybody. And the young towheaded boy, who was now a young hatchet-faced thirteen-year-old, spotted the somber Ingeborg, and he began to scream:

"LOOK EVERYBODY!! IT'S THAT WITCH WHO CURSED THIS TOWN WITH HER WRETCHED HELLSPAWN!! DAMNED FUCKING WHORE-BITCH!! SHE CURSED US ALL!!"

The hideous teen, with the awful penchant for cursing, threw an empty bottle of milk at Ingeborg. It missed, shattering the Barber Shop window she was passing.

This created a stir.

Pedestrians began whispering, curling their necks to exchange their gossip, peering meanly at the scared woman.

Ingeborg was confused, the bottle had staggered her. Even so, she kept walking, looking down and forward and occasionally glancing from side to side at the bitter townies who were emptying into the streets.

It was when she passed the local bar, frequented by miners, that things deteriorated. They piled out of *Jenkinson's Brew* in the tens of twenties.

The men and women, mostly out of jobs and mostly soused, with their faces smeared by the charcoals of a subterranean earth, squinched their acerbic eyes and twisted their pickled faces— directing scorned gazes at Ingeborg.

Ingeborg picked up her pace. She did not care about the groceries anymore. She just wanted to get home, to her daughter, Ingrit, in one piece.

"Ye dumb BITCH!" a drunkard screamed, wobbly at the knee, propped up by an equally deranged brute.

"FUCKING WHORE!!" another yelled.

They began advancing down the street behind Ingeborg.

Others joined too. It became a mob: a stream of dejected persons, roiling and bubbling with a sharp hatred. They blamed Ingeborg for it all, since she had given birth to the "freak" with too much skin.

Ingeborg sprinted down a side-alley and began rushing home.

"KILL EM! FUCKING KILL EM!!" a woman yelled.

"SHE DID THIS, SHE DID THIS TO US!! HER AND THAT ABOMINATION!!" another said.

Ingeborg was pursued by the crowd, an agitated hornet's nest moving with the purpose of violence. The mob grabbed weapons on their way, bats and clubs, and they emptied out bottles and filled them with petrol.

Ingeborg's sides ached as she ran, while she wheezed oxygen into her tired lungs.

Her mind raced in a blurring of frenzied thoughts, which matched her frenzied feet. She didn't know how she could pull her immobile daughter from that dark-damp corner. Her skin was too much. It had grown an unfathomable amount.

Soon—she saw her squat brick house covered in graffiti— surrounded by dry earth. That eyesore needed to become their bastion, a place in which Ingrit and she could hunker down and pray. Maybe the mob would simply get tired and head back to their ramshackle, soot-covered little town after they blew off some steam.

She burst through the door, slammed it behind herself, grabbed some loose boards and began nailing. Ingrit called from the other room.

"What's all that noise, momma!?"

"Don't worry, honey, I'll look out for you. Just don't you worry..." she worked like a woman possessed, battening every opening for the oncoming onslaught.

And soon... they arrived. About two hundred men and women and children, and more were on their way. They were not singular personalities. They were a snarling mass of bitter countenances. And they were screaming and chanting together.

Ingeborg ran into her daughter's room. Closing the door behind her.

She saw her daughter fully now, just an amorphous form made of pallid, rolling flesh with beady black eyes. Sitting in the corner—yet taking up the entire space.

When Ingeborg saw her, she felt nothing but love. A mother's love. For she believed her daughter was beautiful. They both began to whimper and Ingeborg nestled her head into the superfluous skin of her offspring.

"I'm sorry, *momma*," Ingrit wept.

"You did nothing wrong, you're my baby, you'll always be..."

Suddenly, a scream, followed by a crash.

"GET THAT DISGUSTING SKIN BITCH OUT HERE AND WE'LL GET THIS OVER WITH!! SHE SHOULD'VE BEEN KILLED AS A CHILD. SHE'S AN ATROCITY!!"

Ingeborg dug her arms into the loose flesh.

They began pelting rocks and hammering the doors and windows with their clubs. One man yelled, *STAND BACK!* so they did and he chucked a poor man's hand grenade, a Molotov cocktail, at the brick domicile.

Searing flames licked out sidewise, falling onto the dry earth, catching the ground afire.

Before the crowd had a chance to comprehend, they were engulfed. The blaze leapt from figure to figure as though they were kindling brush.

The amount of gasoline and liquor and gunpowder they'd

brought with them facilitated the spreading. The mob shrieked. And their skin dripped onto the soil like melting wax.

Their nerve endings seared, and the fire ate their noses, their ears, their waddles, their weenuses, and their genitals as they sprinted in every direction.

That's what happens when fire envelopes the head.

Even though humans are taught to roll on the ground, instincts kick in, and we run. And some ran back to town.

And it, too, caught on fire. While the little brick house stood, like a flame retardant military outpost, still and small and strong. Ingrit blinked in her dark, damp corner.

"What's happening? What's going on?"

"I don't know..." Ingeborg stood up and peeked through a little aperture in the boarded-up window of the living room.

What she saw was a vast panorama of destruction—a wildfire had ravaged the land and its people, leaving nothing but twisted-up bodies still hissing from the flames.

The smell was terrible and the people moaned as they lay there, in agony, unblinking, since they had no eyelids. Ingeborg returned to Ingrit and smiled.

"What is it momma?"

"I have an idea..." she said.

INGRIT AGREED. She was frightened. But it was worth a shot.

She had never experienced morphine before, and it took a while for it to take effect, since her body was so immense and flowing in every direction, but eventually... she fell asleep.

Ingeborg took her shearing scissors and began cutting at Ingrit's skin, watching as the pleats bent under the pressure of the blades, splitting apart and opening to reveal bubbly, sub epidermal fat. She sliced long swatches off, with little to no blood, and she put the excess skin into a wheelbarrow and carted it out to the field.

She carefully placed the pieces of her daughter's flesh onto the burnt bodies, one by one, while the men and women and children groaned unconscious.

Then, she began sewing, in the still smoky aftermath, her nostrils stoppered up with cotton balls. She worked for a week, without sleeping. Returning to her home to take more skin from a resting Ingrit, then setting out to the field, then to town with her barrow brimming of epidermis.

After countless hours of never ending toil, Ingrit's inner body became visible. She was indeed, a teenage girl. A real person. And yet, it would be trite to say that she was beautiful.

She wasn't. Ingrit was ugly, actually, with a sharp long nose and a gangly and unwieldy build. However, she was a *human being*, despite all the stitches, and, perhaps most importantly, she no longer had superfluous skin.

Her disorder had served a purpose. It had meaning. And she'd never been so happy, or felt so useful.

The townsfolk of Lanesboro healed over time—their new flesh fused to their bodies, giving them a new lease on life. Soon, they were able to get back to work in fields rather than mining.

And soon, they rebuilt the town.

Only their forms were a bit misshapen now. Hideously deformed and horribly discolored.

Their faces stiff and heavily sewed, like leather armchairs. Their backs and bellies and arms and legs were a patchwork of foreign, corrugated flesh.

One could tell that they'd been victims of a serious injury of some kind.

And if they left Lanesboro, they were often ridiculed and treated poorly. They were even the victims of violence, and strangers threw things at them.

The perspective was hard won. They never stopped apologizing to Ingrit and Ingeborg, who were now, the only normal ones there.

SWEETS AND TREATS

In humongous orange bubble letters, the sign, which was supposed to look like twisted-up party balloons, read the following: "CONRAD'S CORNUCOPIA OF SWEETS."

Lommie beheld the jazzy-glowing words for a moment and grinned, dimpling his seven-year-old cheeks. He scampered forward and pressed his little hand to the swinging door and pushed it ajar.

Jing-a-Ling-a-Ling

A tiny brass bell tolled above his head. The store was bright, overwhelmingly so, and on its walls peeped a wide variety of swirling sweets, chocolates, and licorice—hued as though it had been decorated by the great Bozo the Clown himself.

A pungent perfume of malted milk candies and processed sugars suffused the shop, making it alluring to a clientele consisting of children. And it worked.

The sweet shop had been doing quite well. And the shop owner had had many visitors. Only now it was nine in the morning.

The store was completely vacant, save for Conrad E. Billingsley, the proprietor, who looked up from his cash register and eagerly studied the boy as he entered—making note of his size and of his other physical traits.

Conrad noticed that the boy had uncombed, hazel hair and freckles covering nearly the entirety of his face. His shirt was grimy, his small jeans were caked in old and drying mud, and his sneakers were dirty too.

"Why, hello there! What's your name, little fella!?" trumpeted Conrad.

"My name's Lommie..." the boy looked at his shoes then back up again.

"Lommie!? What a fun name! My name's Conrad! And it's a pleasure to make your acquaintance!"

The boy emptily surveyed the shop, seeming to notice the green and red candy canes and the cotton-stuffed elves in random nooks and crannies holding treasure chests, brimming with chocolate coins wrapped in gold foil.

Conrad observed the child and stuck his fat thumbs under his rainbow-colored suspenders, stretching them out, and then letting them go, so they snapped against his plump chest.

Perspiration gathered upon his forehead as he began to carefully make his way around a glass case of candies, which gleamed under his cash register. Conrad cleared his throat, and stuck his hands out to his sides, doing a sort of bow.

"Maybe I should start calling myself Connie? What do you think? Ha-Ha! Like Lommie!? Connie and Lommie! That would be fun! Wouldn't it!?"

"I guess so..."

"Most of my buddies just call me Billings. You seem like a pal! So, you can call me that. Okey dokey?!"

"Ok, mister..."

"So..." Conrad pressed his hands together excitedly. "What brings you to my wonderful world of sweets on this sumptuously fine summer afternoon, your royal Lommie?? Were you looking to sneak an Abba-Zaba bar? Or were you looking to test your molars on an Atomic Fireball? No, I see it now!! You're a BB Bats sucker sort of rabble-rouser? Or maybe a Charleston Chew?"

Remaining silent, Lommie's eyes scanned the room like camera lenses, taking in the treats covering every inch of the colorful shop. The shop owner, Conrad, was nearly dancing in his white dress shoes with the black soles.

He was an odd looking fellow to say the least.

Shaped like an inverted pyramid, the septuagenarian had the skinniest of ankles. His tailored, violet slacks hugged his weird legs all the way up and over his wide waist only to stop above his belly button—making his stomach hang below the beltline of his pants— like he was smuggling a Buick airbag.

His shirt was checkered with tiny cartoons of dominos and beside his rainbow suspenders bloomed a purple plastic flower, which probably squirted water. His plump, old face was adorned with a curled gray mustache, while a halo of dyed black hair ringed his otherwise bald head.

This was all accented by the man's bushy eyebrows, which were also dyed a deep, shoe polish black to match the little hair that he had.

"Or, if you like sours we have Warheads and Pop Rocks, too!"

"I don't know, sir! I'm lost!" cried Lommie. "I don't know where my parents are!"

Conrad smiled wide, crossed his legs and did another theatrical bow. He began shuffling over to the boy and he put his wide hand behind his ear.

"That's ok!" he said. "Your Uncle Connie is magic! See!?" he pulled a Double Bubble gumball from behind the boy's head. Lommie smiled. Conrad lifted his hands up and over his suspendered shoulder, and, like the thespian he was, theatrically clapped twice.

The whistle of a toy train filled the empty space of the candy shop. The boy looked up and smiled, noticing the choo-choo chugging along its tiny tracks which snaked around the multicolored ceiling.

"MAGIC!!" said Conrad. "Now! Let's get you to your parents! Lickety-split!!"

With the zest of a man much younger than he, Conrad began hopping to the front door of his Cornucopia of Sweets, where he gleefully turned the lock and flipped the sign so it read: "CLOSED."

"Can't have any hoodlums coming in and snatching up our candies to appease their sweet teeth! We have to find your parents!! Now, don't we, Lommie?"

Lommie stood silent. The air in the store began to feel different in a subtle, yet dangerous way. It began to smell different too, as if the candies were rotting beneath the sun.

And the train cried out again.

"Oh, no reason to worry Lommie!! Your buddy-ole-pal Conrad

has it all taken care of!! I will have you home and safe and sound and snug as a bug in no time!! I'm a magic person remember?!?"

Conrad began to do a little funny jig, tapping his black soles upon the tile floor. Abruptly, he pretended to slip and caught himself. Lommie laughed.

"Oh! That's the spirit my little friend!!" Conrad approached the boy and placed a hand on his shoulder. "Let's go to my office and call home! I have plenty more sweets squirreled away in there too!!"

"Ok..." said Lommie. The seventy-year-old man began shepherding the small child through the shop—passing the corner of the glass encasement together as they kept walking and entered into a small room, which was nearly hidden to the left of the cash register.

Conrad shut and locked the door behind him.

"We need to focus on finding those parents of yours!!" he said, sitting down on a beaten-red leather chair and motioning to a landline phone sitting on his desk. It was also red.

"Here, why don't you hop up here on my lap and we'll give your house a ring! I bet they're worried sick!"

Lommie nodded, and Conrad placed his fleshy hands under the boy's pits and lifted him onto his lap. He held the boy in place, even though he struggled, and began sliding his hand up his leg to touch his privates.

"DANGER!! DANGER!! DANGER!!" Lommie announced in a robotic voice.

Conrad pulled his hand back. But it was too late. He had already pushed the button. The insides of the boy, which were not composed of bone and blood, but of computing equipment and a series of wires, sprockets, and gears rigged up to a tremendous amount of detonatable C-4 began shifting into place. Everything *clicked*.

The bomb exploded before Conrad had time to speak... *BOOOOM!!!*

Conrad's Cornucopia of Sweets erupted in a torrent of hellfire, incinerating the predator who died with a surprised look on his hideous face.

The windows to the shop exploded, sending innumerable shards of glass tinkling upon the asphalt streets and the door reading "CLOSED" blew wide open and off its hinges.

Down the street, a white refrigerator truck was parked under the shade of a tall oak. It rocked a little from the roar of the explosion. Four men sat in the truck and pumped their fists and pressed on a series of control panels. They shook hands and congratulated themselves on taking out yet another child predator.

"We fucking GOT HIM!!" Agent Tomlinson shouted.

"Woohooo!!! We did IT!!" cheered Agent Mayhew.

"We've got a dozen more of these sickos to eradicate today!! Let's get out of here, now!" said the leader of the bunch.

The van slowly accelerated from its stopped position and a group of twelve more child robots swayed lifelessly in the back of the van.

The other girl and boy automatons, which looked so incredibly human they would deceive the sharpest of eyes, had not been switched on yet.

For they had yet to be delivered.

ALL THE PRETTY, UGLY, HORSES

An ominous clip-clopping issued forth in waves from the hooves of the stampede, pinging back and forth amongst the high canyon walls.

I could see, through my binoculars, that the herd was made up of mutants—with seven bizarrely misaligned eyeballs atop bluish-green heads that strangely had no ears.

The fur covering the rest of their bodies had a reddish hue, closely resembling the strata of the Arizona cliffs surrounding them. And their manes spurted forth hairs in small tufts, like parched vegetation surrounded by endless desert.

I watched them with astonishment. I felt lucky to even get a peek at these altered horses. They stopped to graze on the carcass of a rotting buffalo. Turkey vultures and other scavengers flew or scurried away upon the arrival of the hoofed menace.

"These mutants will eat anything," said Dr. Abraham Foster, squinting into the eyecups of his binoculars, silently adjusting the center focusing wheel.

"Yes," I whispered. "Is it true that they've been feeding on people, Doctor? And where do you think they come from? Mars or something?"

"That, my boy, is the million-dollar question!" he harrumphed with the scientific excitement of a young explorer. And the creatures stopped chewing, while carrion dripped and splatted from their bloodied maws.

"A hive mind…" Dr. Foster mused.

I was too scared to respond. The horses looked around curiously, as if they had sensed our presence within the cores of their disease-infested brains.

"Silence," said the doctor.

A surge of adrenaline heightened my senses. My hands shook. Who knew what these beasts were capable of? Sweat beaded off of my forehead then fell, quietly, onto the dirt. The animals huffed: had they heard my sweat?

One horse nodded its head at another in the group, demonstrating some form of nonverbal communication. The second animal snorted and looked up the escarpment to where the doctor and I were stilly perched. I quickly ducked my head and tried to remember the prayers my nanny had taught me when I was a child.

"It's coming," said the doc. "RUN!"

I looked down the perimeter of the cliff to see the horse scaling the rocks effortlessly with four newly dislocated shoulders. The mutant now looked more like a ravenous primate than a mare.

"GET THE GUN!" I heard Dr. Foster shouting as I was sprinting towards our research van.

"Hurry!" the Doctor reiterated.

The desert can be an extremely bumpy place, which is what I thought right before I tripped on one of the ground's bigger cracks. I was flying through the air for what seemed like an eternity until I clumsily smacked and skipped on the dried mud. My shin bone was now jutting out of my leg: a calcium branch from a flesh-colored tree. I was close to the van. The Doctor was screaming behind me as the creature lunged forward and grasped him in its freakish hooves. I watched the demon horse sink its teeth into the kind Doctor's neck while blood torrented down his dying corpse.

I reached my destination.

I was opening the van door when the horse looked up from its meal, recalling my presence. I shut the door quickly and locked it. I fumbled through the glove compartment for the weapon and threw the first aid kit behind me, then some dirty napkins and some old fast-food receipts. The Glock .40 glowed in front of me. It's lethality momentarily blinded me, like some metal Ark of the Covenant. I turned. And the beast vanished.

The keys kept slipping from my clammy hands that were now shaking like Jell-O. My palms were so greasy with sweat they resembled jiggling crab meat drenched with melted butter. After a huge effort on my part, I was finally able to stick the key into the ignition. I listened with relief as the van's engine awoke from its slumber then rumbled to life. I hastily put the car into drive, then punched my good foot onto the accelerator.

The roundabout road that weaved through the mountains and back to the research lab seemed more menacing now. I compulsively checked my rearview mirrors for any sign of the horse or his friends.

A cascade of tears wetted my eyes. I'm unsure if these tears were from the relentless pain in my leg or from watching my mentor, the great Doctor Foster's throat get bitten into like an apple.

Dusk was heralded by the scarlet skyline with its receding star on the horizon. "What the holy fuck!" I yelled to myself.

The Doctor's oldies station started playing Q Lazarus's techno anthem *Goodbye Horses*. I didn't change the channel, it seemed like too much of a coincidence. The prophetic humming of the automated songster serenaded me into a peaceful epiphany.

He's right... I thought. *I am saying goodbye to these damned horses.*

I drove for delirious hours until the van bumped to a halt in front of the research center. It was night now, and I watched a cloud of dust particles become illumined by the iridescent moon. I checked the rearview mirror one more time, then hobbled from the van. My face twisted in pain.

I knew the only phone that could reach the outside world was located inside, next to some old science magazines and dusty lab equipment. We had cell phones. Nice ones too. However, these Nokias were about as useful as a mirage of an oasis to a thirsty traveler.

The nearest reception tower was more than 73 miles from our decrepit outhouse. I punched in the key code, fighting with a biology that desperately wanted me to pass out. The door beeped then bleeped and then opened slowly as I stepped in. A man was sitting at the good doctor's desk. He slowly swiveled his chair around while I watched in awe. I felt like I was hallucinating from the pain in my leg, it was Doctor Foster.

"Hello, my boy!" he shouted gloriously, a giant hole gaping from the side of his neck. He was pallid and gaunt looking from the loss of blood. He looked dead.

"Doctor... how... what..." he put his hand up to silence me, then dove into an explanation beyond belief.

"You think I'm dead, right?" before I could answer he said, "hardly... those horses made me feel truly alive."

I pointed to his neck. "Oh this, nothing more serious than a mere shaving accident my boy!"

"How are you here?"

"The horses carried me like a young crowd surfer. I was looking up to our glowing moon giddy with excitement to tell you of my revelation."

"What the hell is happening Doctor..."

"You see, I'm different, my perception is different, my everything is altered, it's new, it's boundless."

Even in my state of growing nausea, I noticed an industrious air wafting off the rejuvenated Doctor. The room spun.

"Sit down, dear sir. You need to rest while I explain."

I obeyed, sitting in bewildered compliance.

"A few weeks ago, a local news reporter was called to the scene of Marlowe's farm. The residence was a rustic little Arizona pueblo with a small ranch and some horses. The farm owner, Marlowe, claimed that a meteor had *whooshed* through the night sky and had killed one of his horses. Cut it in half. They showed the carcass. Ghastly sight. However, I digress."

"The other horses had vamoosed, vanished, gone astray into the desert and Marlowe wanted some reimbursement. His profane rant on the local news had to be edited, so it was only a few seconds long, but in short, Marlowe thought that NASA had sent this meteor to his house. Therefore, it owed him for his lost ponies."

My head was bobbing, my vision blurred and the bright lights of the lab seemed brighter.

"I am a scientist... I discern NASA doesn't control meteors. Humans are too imbecilic, too small. However, alien societies more advanced than ours can accomplish what we cannot. Which is, the sending of meteors through wormholes. Why do this? So they can deliver alien organic matter to our pea-brained earth and spark the evolution of our species. They can create new ones and eradicate the obsolete. This is what my attacker showed me. He killed me so I could live! He was Marlowe's stallion, Stan. Now he is so much more. Now I am so much mo..."

I lost consciousness, then woke up with a syringe of adrenaline sticking out of my heart. Everything came into focus, suddenly. I glimpsed the strange, ever-changing Doctor standing across the room, studying some charts. He was scratching his head with a hoof that had replaced his left hand.

This must've happened while I was unconscious. He pivoted around and I noticed a set of giant teeth sticking out of his mouth like busted piano keys. His old hoary head had lost the hair on its sides. Now, in the middle of his head, stood a strange purplish Mohawk that resembled a demented horse's mane.

"Doctor?" I asked, puzzled.

"Yes, yes, yes, yes, yes. Where was I? Oh, yes, our DNA is frighteningly similar to that of horses and the other vertebrates that inhabit our world. The "aliens," if you will, are splicing our genomes to create something spectacular. I see it so clearly now. Humanity is coming to an end, so something new will be in its place... would you like a carrot?" he asked, holding out a bag of the orange vegetables with his remaining human appendage.

"I think you're infected Doctor, we need to get you to a hospital. I need medical attention, too." The misshapen Doctor Foster stared at me for a short while then retorted.

"I will put my saliva into your system, then your leg will be good as new and we can continue the extermination the meteor has started."

Just as he finished, his face opened down the middle and a horse's snout disgustingly emerged. He snorted then evacuated his nostrils spraying a greenish slime all over the lab equipment. My former mentor staggered towards me and I received the strong impression that I was about to be bitten. I reached for my bag, then pulled out the Glock and aimed with tears flowing from my eyes.

"STOP!" I screamed, but the creature kept shuffling forward. I pulled the trigger and closed my eyes until I heard a clicking noise. The clip was empty.

The half-horse-half-man was sprawled out dead before me on the floor of our research center. Dr. Foster was unrecognizable. Something new, something indescribable lied full of bullet wounds in a bloodied heap of lab coat and horse hair.

I spotted the shining ruby telephone on one of the lab's many tables. I was still severely injured, despite the adrenaline. So, I painstakingly crawled, like an overgrown newborn, to the lifeline and unhinged it. I dialed 911. I didn't know who else to call; it was the only number I knew. They had to answer in cases of emergency, even bizarre ones like this. It was a few hours before anyone came. The adrenaline began to wear off while I drifted in and out of a fugue.

They came first in squad cars wearing ordinary police uniforms. The officers were horror-struck and one new cadet named Myerson spewed vomit on our formerly sterilized lab. Soon, helicopters hovered down from the cloudless sky and a specially trained police force rappelled to the ground. Their shoes left boot prints on the alien-like terrain as they stormed the complex. More backup was radioed in. None of these specially trained fighters knew what to make of the fantastic scene. Our outpost looked like something out of the mind of Salvador Dalí.

Eventually, giant military grade trucks arrived with soldiers holding flamethrowers and wearing yellow hazmat suits. I told them everything that the Doctor told me over a hundred times. I was mumbling and fatigued beyond belief, but they kept me lucid with regular doses of steroids and smelling salts.

After I'd told the story so many times, words had lost all meaning, they hovered me out on one of the helicopters. My consciousness shrunk to a small luminous dot, then dissolved. I then, gratefully, received medical attention in a quarantined room of some far-off government base. Maybe I was in the fabled Area 51. I don't know. They told me nothing. Days flew off the calendar like moths plunging from a radioactive bug lamp. I convalesced, ran in circles, and yearned for the day when I would be free.

Months now had passed and I was still in my cell waiting to be released. One morning, I was spoken to by a soft, melodious voice through the overhead intercom of my mandatory habitat. She told me she was a scientist named Marsha. But I don't know if this was her real name.

Either way, she sounded like an angel.

Marsha said matter-of-factly, "The herd of mutant horses is gone now. They've been scorched into a fiery nonexistence. Marlowe's farm and greenhouse have been set aflame as well. You're safe here."

"Yea, thanks, but when can I leave?" I called out.

No one replied. The unfriendly Marlowe, whose horse was killed by the meteor, was quarantined in the holding cell beside mine. I could hear him yelling, constantly saying that NASA owed him his "Mirander" rights. The asteroid, I was told, was in an unknown lab, being analyzed and dissected. I pictured this briefly. Then I asked Marsha, my disembodied savior, if I could have another helping of carrots.

"Of course," she said.

THE BREADCRUMB TRAIL

W hen I heard Mark's nine-year-old girl, Trixie, gone missing I nearly had a heart attack and fell out my chair.

Instead, I spit out my coffee—soaked the whole table. I couldn't believe it. But my wife, Kristeen, told it to me in that sort of way she tells me stuff that she knows is going to be hard to take in.

She's wearing her gaudy, bright, Sunday's best when we gets the call, and she puts down the phone with her eyes more open than anything I could ever word out.

"It's Trixie," she whimpers. "She went missing yesterday and hasn't returned home." She slowly sits down and starts to cry.

I learn that most of the men in our town are going to go look for her in the big expanse of woods bordering our homes. Cause the last place she was seen was down by the archway of spooky old Herald's Bridge.

She was feeding some mallards with a little eight-year-old boy by the name of Teddy.

But Teddy's home safe now and says he and Trixie had splitted up cause she wanted to tread some shortcut through the forest that eventually leads up to her Daddy's estate.

Her Daddy, Mark, is of the more well-to-do of us in Lanesboro— he has a herd of about seventy cattle which he systematically breeds and sells, either for more husbandry or consumption. He's got some other animals, too.

I imagine Mark, sorta the unofficial mayor and proclaimed the blessed one of our town, tearing out his black hair and gnashing his teeth, pounding the walls in his big home while his trophy wife tries to calm him down. And I sees my wife in front of me howling like she lost one of our own.

I get it... my wife's all worked up dithering for a reason. It's not the first time. Many kids gone turned up missing, never to be found again in Lanesboro over the years. An old wives' tale says there's some sorta child-eater in the woods.

I don't believe that though. No God-fearing Christian should give credence to woo woo—way I reckon it.

After a spell of consoling, I head out to meet the others down at the parking lot of Saint Michael's and I hug and tell Kristeen all is *swell* and all is *fine*, that the Lord's done counted every single hair on her little blonde head and that she's probably just lost is all.

That little girl was so sweet, so cute, and just so danged smart. She'd always be riding her bicycle up and down our street, her blonde hair done up in pigtails, and she'd always wave, brandishing those big dewy eyes. I prayed she'd be alright.

Our two boys were a little too old to be friends with her, but the sentiment remained strong.

When I got there, I seen about twelve local fellas of whom I'd known from being around—as it both is and was a small town. Some were holding baseball bats, others were gripping pitchforks or mattocks or holding flashlights, in case the sun fell down too soon while we was still out there.

And I see Mark. He's sobbing and his back is just bopping up and down, up and down. Just like I figured. I never done seen him like that. He's a big man and a proud man and I couldn't help but think that he looked small from all his sorrow and misery.

I tried to hearten him best I could, but he says he just wanted to head out.

And so, we did.

We trudged along a tributary of Root River to where the girl was last seen. And it wasn't long till one of our number spotted the bread-crumbs leading away from the creek-side rocks under old Herald's Bridge.

The bridge was spooky and gray, like an old man's prick, and the whole world had this ominous feel even though it was the brightest of days. But those breadcrumbs, of which someone'd reckoned came from the feeding of the mallards, gave Mark a little hope.

He brightened and puffed up with a new resolve. His black beard bristled in the whispering breeze.

"We're going to find her damnit. And if anyone's touched my little girl, I'm going to rip him limb to limb!"

His eyes were welling up and you could see that behind his bluster existed a whole tiny-universe of worry. Poor, poor, fella. I could barely imagine what he was going through.

Some in town previously thought of Mark as an arrogant sort of businessman, a curmudgeon even, and I'd had a few odd exchanges with him myself—but now I just seen him as a worrisome pa. And I think he was happy to have the company and support of the commu-nity in his time of need.

Donny Irons, one in our lot—an old cowpoke who was comprised of the salt of the earth and the grit of his will said *she must be leaving a sign for us ta folla...* and we all thought the same, it didn't take no scientist, but Donny had been a tracker in the Korean War so none of us made him feel like he was dumb.

Mark kept balling up his fists and rubbing his beard and said: *Come on, let's go now! There will be plenty a time to play with your peckers when you get back to your shacks!* So, we did go, and I was sorta annoyed he talked to us like that, especially Donald, but I figure he's just grieving is all.

Where was I...

We start hoofing it into the tall forest; two big trees served as some threshold between what I used to believe in and what I believe in now while recounting this story. I'll continue...

The forest is made up mostly of sugar maple, American elm, basswood, and some red oak, and we were treading over debris of sticks and bracken and maneuvering over felled logs.

Our noses were near glued to the forest understory, like bloodhounds following this breadcrumb trail.

It's really pretty amazing she left the crumbs behind, I thought. Then I started to think it very strange for a child to do so, but didn't want to tell Mark in his time of bravery and brawn. Because it may be fleeting... his bravery that is.

Say... if he is eventually faced with the loss of his little girl.

I couldn't imagine it. A man would crumble under those circumstances; but I just kept praying and praying and looking down at the little white globs of bread littering the earth's floor and kept trekking deeper and deeper into the woods.

We'd walked for an hour or so, and whenever someone would slow down, as some of us men were older in age, Mark would keep on trudging ahead—the vanguard determined to find his missing daughter.

"Mark, I promise you all is going to be alright," I told him. "She is probably just wandering and done lost her way."

"That ain't like Trixie," he said. "She knows to be home before sunset, for her supper and schoolwork. This ain't like her... none of it is."

Mark started to look crazed and he moved like a puma. I'd never seen him like that neither. He was angry. And worried. I chose to let him alone while all of us observed a meditative quiet, tracing the breadcrumb trail that seemed to go on without end.

I didn't know how much damned bread Trixie had had with her. It seemed weird to me, but I chose to keep my mouth shut, just hoping we would find his girl.

The sun started to set when we were about three hours in and the breadcrumb trail was still keeping strong. It'd teeter off a bit every once in a while. Then it'd spring up again like white moss on the underbrush.

Soon, the afternoon sun was barely filtering through the tall canopy of trees and my feet were starting to get blister sore. One of us clicked on his flashlight. And the others who had them followed suit.

Lighting the way while the bread seemed to *glow*.

When it was all dark out, the noises of the forest seemed more menacing and one of the boys, Russel Chambers (an ex-minister who left the fold cause of adultery), starting humming *Nearer My God to Thee,* while Mark and some others called out for his girl. But no one was answering.

We started to whisper amongst ourselves and some in the group was getting scared cause we thought we heard some wolves. We'd make a sorry lot if a pack of 'em ran up on us in the dark.

Mark wasn't havin' it. There wasn't no turning back for him. And it was his resolve that strengthened us all.

Despite the fact that he kept throwing little deriding-insulting remarks in our direction during the march, but we jus' excused it due to his anxious state cause of his Trixie.

He hit one of the guys in the chest and said, "If it was your little kid out there you know I wouldn't leave you high and dry! Don't be weak!" his stare was mighty deranged and wet with tears and we all agreed with the sentiment; so, we trod on.

About a half hour later, we all started to smell something burning, like spoiled eggs on a stove, and Mark doubled his pace, hollering wild for Trixie. We ran with him and stopped cold in our tracks. The trail led to a small swath of a clearing that led to the mouth of a big, yawning cave.

And we stood there for what felt like a long time, but it couldn't of been more than a few minutes, staring at the bread clumps leading into the aperture. We were all mighty confused, and I'll be the first to admit, that we were mighty frightened as well.

Mark, myself, and the others stood motionless trying to puzzle out just what we were looking at.

"It smells like hellfire," said Chad Meier. And it did. It smelled like Sulphur.

Mark started hollering some more for Trixie, looking into the cave and a few of the fellas held him since he was sorta shakin' and crying. I knew he'd crumble; I would have too, since it was no ordinary cave.

The whole thing was licked with flames on the roof and walls, and the stalactites and stalagmites in the cave were smoldering like coals. The floor of the damned aperture seemed to be made from orange vertebrae and you could hear the pained wallowing of souls within.

"She's fuckin in there! I know it!" cried Mark.

I wasn't in any position to disagree with him—the trail led us straight to the mouth of what looked like hell. But why in the world hell and the devil would take a little girl I wasn't so sure. I began praying the *Our Father,* but was immediately shushed by one in our lot.

"Daddy, Daddy, is that you!! Help me! Daddy!!" a little voice called out.

It was her alright, or at least it sounded an awful lot like her and it was coming from the ungodly sight before us.

"Yes! It's me honey!! Are you Ok!? I come to save you. Tell me that you're Ok, sweetie! Tell me! Please!!"

"I need your help, I'm trapped. Please! Daddy! Hurry!! I'm so scared!"

Mark shook himself free and began to move forward. I put my arm on his shoulder to stop him, just a reflex I guess, but he wriggled free.

"Mark, this could be a setup! I mean, come on! What the heck are we looking at here!? We need to get others! We need to get a priest!"

Mark just set his strong jaw and glowered at me sorrowful like, with tears welling in his eyes. I knew he was going in there, and I knew, from every instinct I had, that if I did, I'd never see my wife or my two boys again.

"Don't try and stop me, none of y'all! I need to get my little girl. I need ta get Trixie! And if none of you cowards are coming with me, then so be it! You're all weak any ways! And dumb as rocks!"

We just looked at the man, shocked he'd say such a thing, but the more I thought of it, he probably didn't want us to follow him. That's why he was saying all these things. He knew it was too dangerous. So, none of us did. We looked on as Mark hardened himself and began walking into the cave holding a pitchfork in his trembling hands.

I swallowed toughly and saw that as he stepped in, the cave howled with the anguished bellow of a thousand souls and we all watched as it suddenly shut behind him. Closing him in! We rushed to the side of the mountain and clawed at the earth, pulling out nothin but clods of soil. He was gone. And we couldn't believe our eyes.

We dug for a few hours...

It was a long, long walk back, and one done mostly in silence. Some of the fellas were shivering and reciting their prayers to all the saints and angels their minds could possibly conjure.

I just recounted the events in my head, over and over again, and promised to keep what I seen to myself. Or to at least write it down, for posterity. As I am doing now.

We split up at the border of town and slowly tread back to our homes. Kristeen was still up waiting for me, but when she saw me, she knew there weren't no good news to be had and just started whimpering and sobbing anew.

I held her for nearly three hours, not bothering to change outta my coveralls, just lied there in bed till she fell asleep, staring at the cracks in my ceiling and remembering the crags and hooks of that fiery cave.

The strange thing was—the next morning, we did hear some good news. Trixie had returned home. To her daddy's estate. She really was just lost and said she knew nothing about no breadcrumb trail.

She was a just little stunned and hungry, but that was bout it. The whole town breathed a sigh of relief since she was Ok and Kristeen immediately started moving about the house and baking up a storm of pies and strudels for her.

It was really somethin', I mean, crazy really.

I kept the specifics of Mark's disappearance to myself, as we all did. Knowing that that hell and those demons or anguished souls were probably out for him, and only him, the whole time.

I mean, he never was too good of a fella. Specially the way he was speakin' to us out there. And I can tell you that I never questioned going to Sunday mass or believing in something more than myself ever again.

Cause, I never knew when a trail would lead me astray as it did to Mark, and I made sure to be extra careful in watching my words and in keeping nice to everyone, and I made sure to never follow no damned crumbs of bread, ever again, for the rest of my life!

AN IMMACULATE CONCEPTION

In a small Serbian cottage, surrounded by the lushness of rolling hills, lightning reached its crackling fingers across the blackness of space, heralding the arrival of a peculiar baby who wailed into the night.

The mother held her son in her damp arms.

A mustachioed Doctor, surnamed Bogdanovic, patted the infant with linen cloths which absorbed the amniotic fluids readily. He stared into the newborn's eyes, big and bright and open, shimmering like polished rubies in a traveling gypsy's bazaar.

"Everything seems to be Ok here," he said. "Don't hesitate to ask if you need anything more."

As soon as the Doctor said the word "more," a tremendous thunderclap resounded outside. The Doctor jumped from the abruptness of the noise and—being somewhat startled—he quickly bade farewell to the people huddled in the cottage.

They pled for him to wait out the storm, but the gentleman politely refused. After bestowing his congratulations upon them, he deftly snapped up the collar of his frock coat, covered his balding head with wooly stitching, and struck out into a drizzling darkness that buzzed with ominous lightning.

His horse was startled, which in turn startled Doctor Bogdanovic further. The animal's whinnies professed some enigma indecipherable to him.

"Why is he freaking out now?" the fine clinician asked himself, calming his steed.

"Chauncey's gone through worse downpours than this. And he usually holds the unperturbed countenance of a statue war pony. Could it be the child?

"Is it not strange that this boy knows no father?" he shivered with the thought. "Did I not have some kind of foreboding before my arriving at this cottage? The skies were blue and cloudless if I remember... where did this storm come from?"

He ruminated within the recesses of his learned brain, only to come to illogical and unscientific conclusions.

"When the contractions started, so did the clouds and as soon as the baby was born, lightning cut across the night's sky. Could he be a demon?"

He mounted his animal, and their respective emotions of unease amalgamated to a palpable fear. With this fear, the horse galloped into the wetness of the stormy night. And Doctor Bogdanovic swore never to return.

THE FOLLOWING weeks were blissfully sublime for the family and their new baby. The mother cherished her child, swaddling him like a pink and cooing gift bestowed from on high. The boy's oldest and only brother whittled him a Pegasus with rubbished tinder.

Meanwhile, in the nearby hills, things were not so peaceful.

The good doctor was visibly shaken upon his rain-soaked return. His dutiful wife was concerned.

It was obvious that something was brewing in his mind and the fearful suspicion that initially gripped him at the cottage only deepened upon his journey home. He told her everything, from the lightning to Chauncey's trepidation to the fact that the woman somehow miraculously conceived without a husband or a lover.

Elsa, Doctor Bogdanovic's wife, placed a warm water-soaked cloth upon his forehead and led him to bed to rest. She was adept at consoling her husband. She also, coincidentally, was the town gossip and in the following weeks, the news spread that the antichrist had been born in their midst.

The townspeople squawked and squealed while the story loomed large in their minds, teetering, ready to crash down upon ignorant sightseers like a tremendous gargoyle.

The anecdote transformed and grew grimmer, as stories often do when the disease of gossip infects the ears.

Some said that this boy was the bringer of destruction and death upon this earth. The great cleanser who would wipe out mankind, leaving only a select few who were fit for holy Christian sainthood. The people counted their sins and squirmed and sweated nervously.

Others said they saw starships hovering above the little cottage: "Just nine months ago, I swear on my own two eyes!"

"I saw them too; there were lights of many colors flashing on the spinning bulbs surrounding their space carriages."

There were differing accounts. Even so, everyone in the village agreed. The strange lady who mostly kept to herself was impregnated by extraterrestrials, or Satan, or a mixture of the two: Satan from outer space. They needed to further unravel the strange case, so the villagers called a town meeting to find out what they could do about the doomsday child.

"I say we burn him before he burns us."

The town's pub erupted in chatter, as though it were filled with deranged apes.

The Doctor stepped onto an elevated platform at the front of the room to address his countrymen. He raised his hands up and soon the old and young maidens started shushing the others. He tiredly dabbed his forehead with his worn-out handkerchief, wiping away the beads of sweat that had gathered there.

"In all my days practicing medicine, and all my time spent in university, I have never come across a case such as the one that lives up on that hill."

He went on to describe the dreadful night where, "instead of life, I helped birth death... the child has hooves and horns like the demon bitch Karakondzula, but it is a boy."

Everyone gasped and a fat man with beer stained breath called out, "It is a male! We don't know what power he will have or what he even possesses now. We need to snuff him out."

The people applauded while their fears swirled around the tavern and mixed into a pungent energy. They were drinking in each other's ignorance and taking shots of suspicion and in their drunkenness, they could not see.

"God will see us through!" the mayor called out while the horde of beasts and bitches and jackal children hurried from the bar.

A small and boney child with a sickening grin was passing out lumber. A man, seemingly his skeletal father, was helping light the wood surmounted with cloth to make torches. The group marched over the moon-splotched hilltops, enveloping the green pastures like crazed ants. They were caught up in the frenzy of emotion and their eyes glazed over with hatred, fanaticism, and madness.

They gripped their clubs while they marched, fueled by the adrenaline of fear, closer and closer to the cottage. Soon smoke started to fill the small dwelling, and the mother was awoken by her eldest son.

"We've got to go, they've come for the baby!" he shrieked, shaking his only parent.

"Here, we can leave out of the back of the cottage," she answered in the midst of survival mode—quickly scooping up the targeted newborn.

"You go first. I'll be right behind you," said the small boy.

He hugged his scared mother and ushered her to a breach in the rotted wall, hidden behind their wooden cupboards. She nodded to her firstborn and crawled in with the baby wrapped in tattered blankets and clothes.

After she crawled a few meters, the boy pushed the cupboard back, then pivoted and charged through the front entrance. She didn't look back, believing he was right behind her.

He was not.

Her son distracted the mob and was fell upon in a matter of moments—being bashed and sliced by the talons of her deranged countrymen; trampled under their hooves of paranoia; sacrificed like a lamb led to the altar so all the bloodthirsty lions could be sated.

She'd mourn him for the rest of her life; she'd never forget his face.

The woman sprinted from the escape hatch with her baby bundled in her arms. Running with abandon, she didn't look back for fear that if she did, the nightmare would become true. When she was almost half a mile away, someone in the ravenous congregation spotted her fleeing form.

"There she is! The woman and her devil!"

The crowd hooted as they pursued her all the way to a steep escarpment of rock, overlooking a churning and foam-laden ocean. She stood with her back to the water, her baby still in her arms. Her trembling legs teetered on the precipice before darkness.

"What do you want!?" she yelled.

"We want that abomination in your arms." The doctor moved forward, still speaking, "We want to throw it off that cliff and we'll throw you off too if you make us."

The mother closed her eyes, tears rolling down her rosy cheeks. She opened them. The crowd was still inching forward.

She swallowed and let herself fall backwards.

The mob became silent. They didn't expect suicide, and they looked around quizzically for some scrap of their lost sanity. They kept moving forward, decisively approaching the cliff's face.

Suddenly, a loud noise, like a googol of trumpets blown in unison erupted from beyond the drop. The multitude recoiled as flashing lights shone upon the bluff and upon the creatures they'd become.

Color ran from their faces.

A ghostly vessel rose high above them, suspended in mid-air. Metallic and silver and spherical. It was spinning while floating— while its hull, simultaneously, lingered eerily still. It hovered there for what seemed like an eternity.

In reality, it was probably a few minutes, or even a few seconds spent judging the fleshy bacteria from its high vantage. Seeing their fangs and vampirically yellow eyes glowing in disbelief.

Then suddenly, the ship floated up a few more feet and zipped into space. A streak of light dissipating into the blackness between the stars. A microcosmic example of their smallness in the universe, had come and gone.

The mob stood in silence for a few moments, until the mayor cleared his throat, and said:

"I guess we found the father."

BEYOND THE CRACKED SIDEWALK

Susan noticed a telephone pole plastered, stapled, and glued with layers upon layers of flyers, varying in shade and hue, beyond the cracked sidewalk.

And she saw, adjoining the telephone pole and the sidewalk, a square of brittle-brown grass. The dry sward led to a wall of concrete blocks, covered with dozens of coats of now fading paint.

A shrine, albeit a small one, sat at the foot of the wall—decorated with snuffed out candles, now melted globs of variform wax, dead flowers, whose petals quaked in the wind like old maids, and a spattering of soggy, deteriorating teddy bears. A single, yet large word was graffitied on the golden wall in runny red paint.

It said: Rejoice!

Susan turned back to the telephone pole, watching the flyers flitting like so many technicolored doves. Inspecting the flyers more closely, she found that they were, in actuality, "MISSING" posters, for the hundreds of children who'd disappeared while passing through town.

Susan swallowed a ball of fear, thinking back on all she'd heard about the place.

The ghost town was notorious in Southern Arkansas. It had an ominous reputation for truancy, while others viewed it as a void-like junction between worlds.

It'd been in the local news many times, always being described as an empty, capacious town where children could hide from parental authorities.

If they wanted to.

If they were still alive.

The town, which was previously called Fairview, consisted of seven hollowed-out factories, their doors crumbling, their windows boarded up with rotten wood. There was also a school, Fairview Elementary. It was a stark silhouette, rising like a skeletal hand from an unkempt lawn.

Susan noticed it as she passed.

It made gooseflesh of her skin.

There was no one in the town, or at least no one she could discern. She'd felt as if she was tiptoeing through an above ground crypt, a mausoleum inhabited by the spirits of wayward children long forgotten.

Besides a sequence of transient shadows, the source of which she couldn't pin down, the streets were completely and utterly abandoned—festooned with spidering fissures that had long since filled with dust. The few homes were either burnt to cinder or were dilapidated beyond repair.

The only true sign of life, human or otherwise, were the teddy bears, the candles, the flowers, and the graffiti. She looked upon the scrawled, somehow sickening word: Rejoice!

Sure thing, Susan thought in response, curling up her fists. *I'll rejoice as soon as we get out of here.*

She wasn't in Fairview as a sightseeing tourist, and this most certainly wasn't a time to praise the lord.

She ripped a stack of the MISSING posters from the wooden beam, paging through them, searching for anyone who even remotely resembled her little sister.

Frustrated, and without any luck, she kept tearing and tearing, until dozens of papers rested in her arms like an abandoned newborn.

Still nothing.

Maybe some of Hannah's friends are here... She kept searching, tearing and ripping away.

She saw no familiar faces, and yet, the MISSING posters proved to be a portal to the past the more she rifled through them. The dates diminished through the decades, until she was seeing the vacant stares of lost children from the 1950s and the '40s.

On a black and white parchment from 1943, a freckled, smudge-faced youth stared back at her. A dangerous *knowing* rested upon his features, an impish look that made Susan shiver and toss the flyer to the sidewalk.

Upset, and feeling perfectly helpless, she slouched in a momentary defeat, leaning her frame against the golden spray-painted wall.

Exhaustion thrummed in her marrow. She'd been worrying about her missing sister for over a month. And even though she'd pleaded, their father wouldn't lend his tin can of a pickup to the search efforts, out of spite.

His drinking had made him mean, and he'd directed most of that meanness toward his youngest daughter: claiming she was ungrateful, even though she was always polite, calling her libidinous, even though she was only eleven.

He'd also said that she worshiped the devil and shunned God. He berated her with all of this, but Susan, ten years Hannah's senior, knew her little sister was an innocent. She was a virgin, as far as she knew, and a do-gooder in the truest sense.

That's why Susan had been walking for two days.

She took in her surroundings, hearing the wind howl through the holes in the bricks in a town where everyone seemed to have slipped through society's cracks. At the bend of the dusty street, a place that once, she presumed, was a bustling intersection, she spotted a Pedestrian Crossing sign.

The sign was defaced with paint, not unlike the acetone-based hues on the brick wall she leaned against. And it was desecrated in such a way that the stick figures therein were walking into the mouth of a faceless beast. The painted-on monster was a black splotch of ravenous excess, with fangs indicating a bottomless appetite.

It frightened her—she remembered stories about this place, about how the crops almost a century before had withered and died. And how everyone left in droves, saying it was a doomed plot of land, in a town that never should've been. And she recalled hearing about those that stayed behind, how they were never heard from again, or seen. No one knew if the cause of their disappearance was an isolating madness, or if they'd no voices to speak with, other than the wind.

She shut her tired eyes and shivered, lulling into the chasm of sleep.

Above her slumbering head, the sun didn't seem to set, but rather to cool and to smolder, changing into an invisible ball of nothingness that was blotted out from the night's sky by its own inability to burn alight.

THE NEXT MORNING.

A tumbleweed scratched its way through the abandoned streets, bumping into corroded walls, moving here and there like a blind man searching for sight.

The tumbleweed brushed up against Susan's leg, lightly scratching her skin, and as she awoke and pushed it away, she heard something akin to a parade. Her every motor function locked up, stiffening her huddled frame in the radiant morning glow.

Her heart throbbed in her chest, while every one of her every pore's felt flushed with such immense dread. She didn't know why. And then. They came.

Before Susan even realized what was going on, or had the sense to stop it, she'd been encircled. As helpless as an ensnared rodent, and feeling like one—lost in this town of the missing, bunched up into herself, with nothing to do but to note the strangers who circumvented her.

They were all children.

They edged in closer, constricting their circle like a big noose, making her feel as if she were drowning on the musky air of the town.

First, they tread a few feet away, and then, in the smallest flicker of an instant, they came face-to-face, in the strange impromptu meeting of displaced runaways and a lone pursuer.

"H-HANNAH!?" Susan shouted out in a timorous quiver.

The assembly didn't respond, at least, not in the normal way of children. They hissed like nests of vipers. So, she became quiet. Determined to protect herself as best as she could, pulling her legs in close to her sternum, as her trappers closed in even further, their dirty sneakers now touching her own.

Fuck, she thought.

And with fright puncturing her spine, she observed.

WHAT STRUCK SUSAN, were the sheer amount of kids present, none of whom seemed older than twelve. What occurred to her next, made her swallow an anxious lump. She'd seen one of the children before, or at least thought she had.

He was identical to the boy from the 1940s MISSING poster, the one she'd ripped from the wooden post. He was now two-inches from her face, reeking like dirt and old sweat. And still seemed to be nine-years-old.

Without warning, and with a force unbefitting of their small statures, countless little hands gripped Susan's arms. Yoking her up to her feet, the children looked on with filth-clad and soot-covered faces, with their hair matted and uncombed, with their clothes resting on their emaciated builds in tatters, barely conjoined by a series of unraveling gossamers.

The thing, however, that made Susan's knees wobble to the point of buckling as she beheld all the faces of the forgotten children, was their eyes—their poignantly haunting stares.

Menacing and inhuman, they resembled chips of slate.

She noticed, too, that they numbered in the hundreds, maybe thousands—their energy like a metastasizing ball of static.

And in that throng she searched for her little sister, pure, innocent Hannah. She didn't see her in the assembly, but she spotted a few others, who'd disappeared from her hometown when she, herself, was a youth. They, like the boy from the flyer, were still the same age.

The child from the 1940s missing photo edged forth, moving in front of the hundreds of whispering others. The boy remained silent, his mind whirring under his ginger hair.

He studied Susan, looking her up and down, drinking her in, contorting his grimy, cherubic face, as if possessed by the ghosts of all the misbehaved children who ever have, do, and will, exist.

Another of the children, a small girl with a blue bibbed and bonneted ankle-length pilgrim dress, shuffled forward, carrying a milk crate amid the conversing crowd. She set it in front of Susan, beside the boy.

Climbing onto the milk crate, the freckled child lifted his hand in the air. Collective murmuring was heard from the crowd before it fell mostly silent, save for a couple of children, who were shouting their hearty encouragements.

The kid gave a coy nod, then an impish grin, waiting for them to join the others in silence.

In the bright light of day, he seemed a little less menacing, and almost angelic. A siren began shrieking from an indiscernible distance, five or ten blocks away, Susan guessed. And she watched as the kid placed a bullhorn to his face, pressed his finger to its button, and started to speak.

"We have here, my friends, my fellow younglings, yet another of the adult world, trying to force us to 'grow up!' To them we scoff! We've left our homes for a simply put reason: escape!

"The adult world never understood us, never allowed us to enjoy youth uninhibited. It treated us as sideshow freaks, we were beaten and abused. The ringmasters manifested illusions, with duplicitous sleights of hands, spun webs of lies, with tongues of deceit! But we've found another way, oh have we!"

The boy gesticulated like a tyrant from his milk crate while the crowd erupted in cheers, hurrahing the escapade with a cacophony of approval.

Enfevered, the throngs swayed as the alarm continued resounding through the emptied thoroughfares. The noise reminded Susan of an air raid siren—specifically, the ones she'd witnessed in the war movies her father was so fond of.

The shrill, ceaseless clamor felt as if it were burrowing into her ears, painfully traversing the canals, then penetrating into the folds of her brain. The world became blurry and hopelessly ill-defined.

Susan had nowhere to run to, she was center-stage with her back to a brick wall. Fleeing was not an option; she had no idea what these ill-begotten cretins were capable of. Swallowing her last ounce of courage, she called out to the mass, for her sister, once more, "HANNAH!?"

The boy from the milk crate grinned with pitted teeth plagued by cavities. It was the inevitable result of no adult supervision. His smile seemed the equivalent to an executioner's axe being brought down upon Susan's neck. She was standing at the shrine, between the series of unlit candles, wilted flowers, and moist teddy bears. She found herself on an altar, in the gallows. The piercing noise seemed to grow in frequency, Susan wept, but nobody noticed or cared. They were too busy laughing.

From a side-street alleyway, adjoining this one like a tributary does a river, came an added procession of children. They were hooded in scarlet cloaks the color of blood with faces obscured by the overarching shadow of their cowls. One youth was leading the march. Behind him or her, walking abreast, side-by-side, in two single-filed lines, were the others. Humming and chanting.

The multitude of children, in reverence to something inexplicable, split and made way for the lingering line of the others to pass. It was tantamount to Moses, parting the Red Sea, yet different, in that this leader of this specific procession, parted its obstacle without so much as an utterance.

The line drew closer. The boy standing on the milk crate jumped up and down, jittering with enigmatic excitement. It was a peculiar, almost savage exhilaration, afforded to him by an inner wellspring of insanity.

Susan could hear the child remarking through gritted teeth, "YES, YES, YES!"

She ignored him while the leader of the line inched forward, and then looked up, meeting the gaze of Susan, unveiling the once furtive identity. She'd found who she was looking for. "Hannah!" Susan yelled excitedly, calling out for her sister, seeing her gentle face as a life raft, buoying her amidst this sea of turmoil and confusion.

Hannah drew back the hood hiding her chestnut tresses, and glared at her older sister, her rescuer, with eyes like knobs of varnished oak. "Hannah, it's ME!" Susan said, bewildered, crying. "What is this? What's happening?"

Hannah remained stoic, letting little to no humanity sully her face. She seemed a porcelain doll, pasty of complexion, and with a novel, austere expression. One Susan had never before seen.

"I told you not to follow me," Hannah said coolly.

"I came to get you, you're my *sister* Hannah!"

The small boy on the milk crate began chortling, then doubled over and began slapping his knee. The crowd, however, remained silently prayerful.

"I'M NOT GOING HOME! I'M NOT GOING BACK THERE! NOT WITH HIM!" Hannah was speaking more severely now, quivering at the tortured remembrance of her father.

"It will be different from now on! I promise! He's not going to lay a finger on you anymore, he just gets drunk is all, that's why he's violent. He's had a hard life," as Susan spoke the words, she knew she didn't believe them. Their father was truly a monster, and he seemed to take out all his frustrations on the easiest target, his youngest daughter.

A single tear rolled over the round, white cheek of Hannah. "I never wanted any of it, even though he said I did. He shouldn't have done that, he shouldn't have touched me there... They'll protect me now," said Hannah, with a voice full of shame, tinged with remorse.

"What? I'll protect you, I promise..." Susan said, realizing what her father had done was far worse than she'd imagined. "Who are these kids, Hannah?" she pleaded.

Her eleven-year-old sister unsheathed a twisted dagger from a fold in her cloak.

"You should've done more to protect me when I needed it," she said. "These kids are my family."

Hannah lunged at Susan, who, ultimately flabbergasted, didn't evade her. She didn't try to dodge, she didn't parry, as the gnarled blade plunged into her gut.

Blood streamed over her fingers and she folded over, bending in two. Quiet filled the town—the siren ceased blaring.

Susan looked up at her little sister, who was crying now, flushed with emotion.

"Here, no one can take my childhood! I'm not going back! NEVER!"

Before Susan could respond, she was stabbed once more, then, repeatedly, feeling the cold blade puncture her organs and scrape against her bones.

She wilted like a chrysanthemum as the shrine's withered roses sprung into full bloom. Breathing her final breaths, garbling on her own fluids, her tear-streaked, sanguine-tinted head rolled to the side, witnessing the audience of runaway children, humming and singing.

Blood inked, then pooled in amorphous puddles around her, while the candles abutting Susan's body suddenly roared alight, gleaming bright and brilliant with glowing, sputtering flames.

The wicks had caught fire, inexplicably, as if energized by the immolation. And the children's faces were illumined by their yellow light. They inclined their eager frames, smirking collectively, in a fashion that seemed wholly demonic.

The last thing Susan saw, as the darkness overtook her, were the ubiquitous smiles. The predatorial fangs of the children. She closed her eyes to shut them out before her untimely death. She tried to speak and call out once more for Hannah, but no plea escaped her lips, for her vocal cords were severed.

The audience cheered, approaching then hugging a mournful Hannah in droves. Susan's little sister was weeping as they embraced her. Limply, she dropped the dagger from her hands. The blood of the cadaver flowed freely now, filling the cracks of the sidewalk, repainting the strange sacrificial altar.

The miscreant, from atop his milk crate, his freckled face pocked with boyish dimples that should've belonged to an eighty-year-old, looked at Hannah.

"We're reborn, once more, never growing in age, never answering to adulthood, or its lackeys, and it's through the blood of your sacrifice. You have pledged us your loyalty. You are safe now, Hannah."

He put a grubby hand on her shivering, cloaked shoulder. Suddenly, the fear and the guilt drained from her, as easily and as readily as water from a fragmented jug. She felt reborn in the blood sacrifice of her sister, suddenly rejuvenated, and all the baggage, the hurt, the remorse, the shame, were no more.

The maleficent influence of adults, of her dad especially, and the unhelping Susan, were suddenly cast asunder. Hannah beamed a smile so wide that the boy momentarily flinched.

"Would you do the honors?" he asked his new pledge. She nodded.

Hannah knelt down beside the corpse of her sister. With sorrow for what she had just done, and the scars of her old life, a distant memory.

"I told you not to follow," she reiterated. She ran the tips of her fingers across the bloodied heap of Susan. Searching for her murderous incisions: when she found them, she wetted her palms and hands.

Hannah stood upright, walked to the golden spray-painted wall, and with her sister's blood, retraced the word: Rejoice! It shone in crimson glory. The audience went insane with celebration as waves washed through them, reviving their bodies, reversing the aging process, making it stand completely still, in a place without time, without growing up.

The teddy bears were no longer dampened — they were full of fluffy, voluminous fur. Hannah looked at them longingly, with the final semblance of maturing hesitation. The freckled nine-year-old perceived her interest, picked one of the bears up, and handed it to her.

Previously, she would feel ashamed to want to hug a stuffed animal. Her father would've told her to act her age, to be a pure, God-fearing woman. Now, she felt reborn, her youth felt protected in the spiritual plexiglass case of this forgotten town. She grabbed the teddy bear, hugged it, and smiled.

A FEW MONTHS LATER, the children who never aged spied and strode, running through the alleyways and unknown passages of Fairview. They soon spotted a young child of elementary age, lost, sniffling, ambling with a branch suspended over his left shoulder wherein his every earthly possession hung within a red bandana.

From the hollowed-out buildings, from the mounds of ash that once were homes, from the crumbling-jobless factories, beyond the cracked sidewalk, they briefly paused their games of kick-the-can and hide-and-go-seek, to welcome a new inductee to immortality.

INTERGALACTIC SATAN

The streets converged in a mass of differing mannerisms and lifestyles—people walking with down-turned heads, wearing surgical masks, drunkenly looking for places to deposit their salaries, posing for pictures with individuals dressed as anime mascots, chitchatting with prostitutes, winding round and round the bustling stream that flowed and went and renewed itself in the warm Tokyo midday.

Enki clutched Ayami's hand, feeling her softness warm the center of his torso in a wave that washed down to his loins. He pervertedly smirked, pulling his plain-blue baseball cap down snugly, so it wouldn't fall off in the bedlam of Shibuya Crossing.

The couple wriggled through a sea of arms and legs, pushing their way around those mindlessly milling and snapping pictures by the Hachiko dog statue.

Hachiko was a dog who, legend has it, waited for its owner to return from work at the Shibuya Station—not knowing its owner had died, the mutt sat and licked its nether-region and whined for many mournful and introspective years—eventually succumbing to old age itself, after a decade had passed.

Hachiko was honored and idolized for its intense loyalty. Everybody loved Hachiko—besides Enki. *The dog was a fucking ragamuffin! If only they could see what its true intentions were!*

He thought differently of the dog, mainly that it only stayed at the station because *blockheads* were giving it food. And it never went home because it had a roof over its head.

Lost in thought about how much he hated Hachiko and his falseness, Enki heard a plump Wisconsinite say, "What a wonderful pooch!"

Stupid Americans, he thought to himself, and bunched Ayami in close.

They just had to get to the station, then they could escape this pattering freakshow in this gaudy area of Japan that many considered special.

Everything was neon-drenched and radiating. High-tech skyscrapers buzzed with advertisements for Sony, H&M, Hisamitsu and Samsung as if Shibuya Scramble Crossing were alive, and the streets were its veins, and the people ever-flowing were its blood.

And... as Enki and Ayami forced their way through the amorphously blathering crowd, a small red flame opened up the sky. The object roared and time seemed to stop—thousands of feet ceased their movement as scores of heads peered skyward. A flaming disc came careering down, crashing in a thunderous explosion not far off in Shinjuku City—then skipping.

The craft leveled buildings as it metallically *clicked* and *clanked,* flipping in a fireball-blur, murdering thousands as it did so. The city screamed. Traffic collisions and explosions manifested aplenty and the roar of once-sleek edifices crumbling to the ground filled the air.

Eventually, as Enki gripped his girlfriend's hand, the crimson UFO tore into Shibuya Crossing, parting the asphalt as it came.

Clouds of dust thickened the air, making it hard to see anything at all through the deep, gray fog, but the pulsing red glow of a flying saucer. Enki screwed up his eyes and listened as the spacecraft hummed, while innumerable mechanisms whirred within.

With the passing of a few seconds, the saucer sprouted six legs and rose noisily from the ground. Most ran, trampling one another. Others held a far perimeter and watched as a red tongue extended from the craft and a small door slid open.

"*What in the hell...*" Enki whispered, smelling a sudden, pungent odor of sulfur.

One hoof, then two, came clicking onto the walkway. And soon, as the dust settled, the extraterrestrial was fully visible, and completely red.

It had the lower body of a goat, yet its upper body was anthropomorphic-looking, and from its dark scarlet sides sprung human-looking arms. One of which clutched a ruby pitchfork while a bifurcated tail swished back and forth behind its body. It sneered, baring fangs from within the circle of a black goatee.

The head of the creature was disproportionate in comparison to the rest of its body. It was humongous. And its eyes were as black as buttons chiseled from onyx and were sunken into its face, just below a forehead that was ridged like a sickly fingernail. It was horned and hideous.

"Come! We have to go! Now!" Enki shook his girlfriend.

Ayami was in a state of shock, but she eventually snapped to and followed Enki into the stream of fleeing pedestrians. The visitor's eyes gleamed devilishly. It outstretched one of its arms and began spraying the crowd with red currents that caused everyone to stand still and sort of jitter.

Enki looked over his shoulder, seeing the electricity accelerating, jumping from person to person, and he suddenly tackled Ayami, pulling his love and himself behind the Hachiko dog statue.

The currents zipped past, rendering most others incapacitated while the couple hugged each other and shook. They watched as the electricity subsided in a series of fizzling sparks that hissed from Japanese bodies and disappeared into the still-smoky ether.

The people gradually stopped spasming—letting out a few strange groans—and they began to glare at one another while the Intergalactic Satan peered from the walkway-perch of his UFO; deviously grinning.

"*Shh! Shh! Shh!*" Enki pressed his forefinger to his lips. Ayami couldn't stop trembling.

"*Get ready to make a run for it...*"

A collective scream—the crowd had morphed into something sly and conniving, their innermost selves gripped by the most perverse of their vices and the most deplorable of their instincts.

Enki pressed his girlfriend to his chest. A police officer unholstered his pistol and began firing into the multitude; no one minded the bullets lacerating and putting holes in their flesh—they were tending to their own sick wants, now unconcealed and in the open air.

Groups of people started humping each other, moaning like nymphomaniacs, and Ayami yelled as some American tourist woman began stabbing an old man in the neck with a ballpoint pen. The old man stared mindlessly into the distance, screaming racist comments about the Chinese.

"NOW!" Enki pulled Ayami to her feet, and they began sprinting through the fighting-humping-robbing horde. A small boy ran up behind Ayami and snatched her purse, saying, *"HAND IT OVER YA BITCH!"!*

He was six years old and was dressed in a tiny sailor's suit. She screamed and let her purse go. Enki held her back, and they watched as the child disappeared into the deranged mass.

"I had e-everything in *there...*" whimpered Ayami.

"Come on, we need to keep MOVING!" Enki tugged his girlfriend by the arm, pulling her into an adjoining alleyway.

And they ran.

Leaping over trash cans and narrowly skirting around dumpsters, the couple eventually expelled themselves a few streets over.

Enki noticed a very familiar izakaya pub called the WAKABAYASHI, known for its sake, prostitutes, and salarymen. And he pointed, and they went, pushing the door open and stepping inside, desperately fighting to calm themselves and to take a breath.

"*Tee-hee-hee!!*" a little voice twittered.

Ayami shrieked, so Enki sidestepped in front of her, shielding her from the ghastly portent of things to come.

A young woman, dressed as a blue Tamagotchi turtle, was

holding a butcher knife and was plunging it into the back of the bartender.

The victim wouldn't stop drinking; he was crying and refilling his beers at the tap and chugging them down till he began hollering and spitting up blood and eventually keeled over dead, a sanguine yeast-like substance foamed from his mouth. The turtle-woman giggled.

"DON'T COME NEAR US!"

The rest of the barflies were stiffening corpses; their fates hinted at by the long brushstrokes of blood and bile recently splashed upon the bar's interior.

The girl, focusing in on the couple, started clambering over the bar. So, Enki snatched up a barstool and brained her with it. She fell crosswise, toppling to the ground—pulling liquor bottles down with her, which exploded onto the bloody floor.

There, she twitched, and her eyes glittered madly for an instant. Her skull had been staved in—yet she smiled.

"She's still *ALIVE!*" screamed Ayami.

"LET'S GO! There's a hotel nearby, we can hole up in there for a while..."

The pair spilled into the street again, seeing cars colliding and spinning out. The drivers, as demented as the rest, leapt from their vehicles and began battling—as though they were samurais in a parallel history that never should've been.

They circled round a writhing pile of thirty or forty citizens, screwing and fellating one another feverishly, while moaning in ecstasy, and they narrowly dodged two businessmen thwacking each another with their briefcases.

A door swung open, and an angry Itamae, or sushi chef, stormed bandy-legged onto the sidewalk. He was wearing the traditional garb, all-white and buttoned, and had on the customary teppanyaki cap. He was holding his sashimi knives akimbo, while shouting something about bad fish.

He began sprinting at the couple. Reflexively, Enki shoved Ayami behind a telephone pole, then began dodging the blades.

Pressing her small hands to her mouth, warm tears glossed

Ayami's porcelain face as she began to rock to and fro, in a panic-stricken-sorrow—which was rather fortuitous, for in that moment, a boot swished past and missed the crown of her skull.

It was the cop from earlier, and he was seemingly out of bullets. The sashimi knife sliced into Enki's bicep and the Itamae screamed. Above, in the distance, a little red devil could be seen, floating on some unseen force, deriving immense pleasure from the madness below.

Ayami shrieked and the cop went to kick her again, so Enki forward rolled in that general direction, grabbing her by the arm and pulling her away.

For a moment...

The sushi chef still advanced, and so did the policeman, sandwiching the couple in between. Enki was slashed across the stomach, while the officer removed his baton and raised it high above his head, sneering, and *BOOOOOOM!!!*

The whole of Tokyo was distracted, albeit briefly—for the dark skies parted like curtains, letting a celestial light overtake the city. Enki and Ayami started running to the Super Hotel Ueno-Okachi-machi, some kilometers away.

When the cop and the chef looked back for them, they were already gone. So, they turned on one another: clubbing and slicing till all the insanity ebbed from their bodies, till they lay bloodied and broken and dead.

THE COUPLE SPRINTED into the Okachimachi as another vessel rocketed, and then gracefully floated, toward the raging cityscape. The receptionist, Kimura, stood placidly and contentedly behind the front desk of his hotel, thumbing his way through the latest edition of the periodical, Yomiuri Shimbun.

Hearing the clamor, Kimura glanced up...

"Hello, how may I help you?"

"THE WORLD'S FUCKING LOST ITS BRAINS OUT THERE, MAN!!" screamed Enki.

"IT'S TRUE!! HE'S NOT LYING!!" added Ayami. "THE DEVIL DOESN'T COME FROM DOWN BELOW! IT COMES FROM OUTER SPACE!! IT'S AN INTERGALACTIC SPACE SATAN!!"

"I get it! This is a gag! Amusing. I have to say. Now, please... our hotel is for paying customers only."

"This isn't a gag!" Enki clenched his fists. Tears poured from Ayami's eyes, she couldn't bear to look at Kimura, who adjusted his nametag, and set his small shoulders.

"You're a little too young to be drinking... Do you need me to call someone?"

"You're insane!" bawled Ayami, clawing for the man's name tag over the granite barrier. Enki grabbed her, trying to calm her down.

"Ok, Ok, fine! Ok. Do you have any vacant rooms?"

"Hmm... I don't assume you have a credit card?"

Enki began fumbling with his pockets, which were blood soaked from the gushing wound across his slashed stomach. Ayami turned away, dropping her head into her shaky hands.

"I'm sorry..." Kimura straightened his posture and impishly smirked. "As I *SAID BEFORE*, the hotel is for paying customers only."

"*No, no, no, I have one!!*" Ayami wheeled around, proffering her mother's blue Visa credit card—which was to be reserved for cases of emergency, of which this most definitely was.

Kimura's shoulders sagged in defeat.

"Alright then, let me look..."

He nudged his glasses up the bridge of his tiny nose, which was exfoliated nicely, then commenced fiddling with the keyboard on his computer. The couple peered around like bug-eyed deer, seeing nothing but a vacuous lobby.

Kimura muttered to himself: *hmmm-eehhhh-ahem-hrrrmm,* then, as Ayami was hyperventilating and pulling her hair, while Enki wobbled, he said: "Yes. We have a room."

"We'll take it!!" the couple blurted out.

Kimura twisted up his face... "I must warn you, the room is very expensive, about 550 yen!"

"Good! Do that!!" screamed Ayami, and the little man shrugged.

He swiped the credit card.

Then, he maneuvered at a persnickety slow clip; the couple embraced, and Enki pleaded: *Come on! Come on! Come on!!*

As soon as Kimura presented the room keys, Enki snatched them up and the two rushed away. Kimura watched them and pleaded for them not to run, but his voice was cut off by a rumble outside.

The receptionist turned his attention to the door, and a deranged lunatic dressed like a Tamagotchi turtle marched in. She had a santoku sushi blade protruding from the forehead of her already bashed-in skull.

"OH, MY, LORD!!" yelled Kimura. He grabbed his walkie and radioed for the hotel's custodian, to no response. "WHY IS NO ONE PICKING UP!?!" he screamed.

Grabbing his newspaper, Kimura then cowered under his desk.

THE ELEVATOR SOARED UP and up, beeping all the way till it reached the thirty-second floor, and its metal doors *swooshed* ajar.

The couple limped into a toffee-beige hallway bathed in fluorescent light and they labored forth and into the costly suite, whose living room was festooned with the highest of high-tech appliances—including a very small flatscreen TV, a teensy-tiny microwave, and a Lilliputian toilet confined to a crawl space of a bathroom.

The "suite" was actually a one-room habitation, with every furnishing piled on top of every other furnishing and appliance for reasons of economic frugality.

The receptionist, Kimura, had duped them. But it was the last thing on either Enki or Ayami's mind, for they saw, out of a very modest window, shaped like the most boring of squares, a craft landing smack dab in the middle of Meiji-dori Avenue near the JR Yamanote subway tracks.

This craft was different from that of the Intergalactic Satan's—for it was much grander in size. About the height of a building. And while the space devil's UFO was blood-colored, this one was pearlescent in hue and was shaped like a giant cross instead of the archetypical saucer.

Ayami sat on the neatly made bed, which was close to the window, since everything was close in the room, and her mouth opened slightly as she murmured the words, *"No way..."*

Enki dripped puddles of blood onto the floor. But... he didn't care. He was too consumed with the external happenings and too wrapped up in the possibility of humanity's end. The space Satan zipped by the couple's window, tapping it twice in rapid succession with the triangular tip of its tail and it landed at street level not far off.

Enki watched the *thing*, as if it was some all-powerful fire ant— its cleft hooves clomping upon the hellscape it'd created, and its ginormous head bobbing, bare of hair save for a goatee, absorbing all of the malodorous malice it'd incited in the murderous-libidinous-gluttonous-dipsomaniac horde of humans, foreigners and non.

The new craft eclipsed the little devil, but the devil didn't seem worried in the least. It simply continued its clomping as the multitude plundered and pillaged around it.

Then...

The cross began to open to the sound of hissing hydraulics, and the whirring din of extra-planetary gears shifting their composite parts—which were made of elements still unknown to humanity and still absent from any reputable periodic table.

Fortunately, the nook of a penthouse the couple had purchased was the perfect place to watch the transpiring scene. Enki sat beside Ayami, painfully; he shivered and he pressed on his wounds. And they held one another.

The city this far up, as down below, looked incredibly effulgent and beautiful, as though it were a metropolis not of this planet— and it was sort of pleasant being out of earshot to the death cries of its citizens.

For a moment, the lovers felt at peace.

And when the door to the monumental cross was finally open, an alien that was about twenty stories in height exited and stepped into the Tokyo bedlam.

The creature was difficult to look at, since it was so radiant it blinded, like the snapshot of a photographer's bulb, that never ceased blazing. The couple winced and held their eyes.

But Enki had gotten a good look at it... and it was oddly shaped, all-curving without muscle or facial-features with two cerulean-blue eyes and a blissfully smiling, lipless, mouth.

"Is that supposed to be Jesus or something..." Enki rubbed his eyes.

"I don't know... I think it has tentacles..." said Ayami.

Before Ayami had a chance to continue, the tall alien began speaking.

Its voice sounded like the synchronous tooting of a million trumpets, indecipherable and horrible to listen to. Suddenly, the little-red-space-Satan began floating up from the ground and it hovered face-to-face with the elongated space-Jesus.

The Jesus-thing outstretched its arms and began filling the streets with a milky light and the people marauding below started to calm and be pacified; and they fell in their places, and stared at one another, stunned and disgusted and asked: *What have we done!!?*

The Intergalactic Space Satan didn't seem to like this, for he propelled himself at very high-speeds into the Space-Jesus' throat, or where its throat would be if it had a throat. And the giant alien flailed backwards, crushing buildings and killing many people.

The couple squeezed one another as the space Satan buzzed within a cloud of red electricity.

The tall alien then floated up, as if resurrected, and it ascended into the sky. The devil zipped after it and they began fighting in the clouds. Sonic explosions of interstellar energy shook the panes of the hotel room's window, as the things pummeled one another and flipped and expelled currents of differing frequencies at one another.

It seemed... the two aliens weren't friends. It was a true clash of the titans. And it was an amazing sight.

"Let's get you bandaged up," said Ayami.

"*But... what about them...*" Enki asked, meekly.

"Oh, I don't think it has anything to do with us. It's between them, and they've probably been doing this for ages."

ACHOO

S arah and Chris Mitchell looked deeply into one another's eyes. A spark, a gleam—from auburn and blue irises respectively—their pupils dilating, their pulses quickening. After five years of marriage, they were still madly in love.

"So... should I buy this dress or not?"

Sarah did a little curtsy, then brought her petite hands beside the black and white sundress, pinching the sides and fanning it out—as if this would change the pattern, as if Chris would look at anything other than her chestnut eyes, her adorable dimples, her heavenly smile.

"Ah, yeah... you look beautiful!"

"You're an idiot, Chris Mitchell!" Sarah smiled coquettishly, then moved to the front desk, a brunette dream.

"If I buy this, can I keep it on?" she asked.

Chris didn't hear the cashier; he just saw her lips flexing into O's so she could better grunt her consonants. He didn't care, anyway.

A love like theirs comes only a few times a generation, it's like winning the cosmic lottery, and Chris spent his time basking in its amorous jackpot. He was smitten by his wife, had been since he first met her over a decade ago.

Their life together was pretty happy.

That's not to say it had all been a breeze, they'd been trying for a baby for years. Sarah, according to the obstetricians, was barren. She'd been that way ever since the two were in college.

"You have structural problems in your reproductive system. Possibly endometriosis... or some such fallopian anomaly. You're most likely infertile. It would take a *miracle*," they said.

So... Chris bought his beautiful wife clothes, and shoes, and took her to farmers' markets, and happy hours, to distract her from the existentialist thoughts women sometimes experience concerning the meaning of life without kids.

They'd keep trying anyway, sex was a favorite pastime of both.

She returned in the black and white dress, beaming. The joy would only last a little while until she started thinking about *life* again.

"Ready?" asked Sarah.

"Yep, let's get going," Chris smiled.

They passed through the store hand in hand, both happy... Chris for the fleeting moment when Sarah was fulfilled; and Sarah, for the seconds in which she forgot her woes.

The door to the irrelevant shop swung open; the two exited and began walking the streets of Georgetown—joyous lovers basking in the springtime sun. Life was simple then.

It was a busy early afternoon. A jazzman blew sultry melodies from his saxophone on the intersection of M and 33rd Street; taxis, buses, cyclists, drivers, all wove in and out from lane to lane in an endlessly dangerous dovetailing dance; horns blared; laughter boomed; people yelled, people fought, people walked with their heads turned down, eyes solemnly transfixed on the heels of the stranger's shoes before them.

The sidewalks, on which Sarah and Chris now walked, held a regular smorgasbord of faces, grinning, drooped, and grimacing. They flitted by and by.

But it was one face, in particular, that stuck out from the rest. Like a bright purple jellybean in a sea of white speckled cotton candies. It was different. Contrasted. Hideous. Grotesque even.

It belonged to an old, old, anciently old woman. She must've been in her nineties, and she moved very, very, slow. She was almost animatronic in her herky-jerky meandering.

The crone had a slender, gnarled, hooking nose, with knobby calcium deposits as though it had been broken many times. Her eyes were beady vortexes to cold, unfeeling nowhere.

She wore a shit-colored shawl. Her face was so wrinkled she looked part Shar-Pei. And her hunchback seemed to have mutated or metastasized in an attempt to break free from her otherwise feeble frame.

The old woman wore a long, drab, green, orange, and purple denim looking skirt. And her feet slid across the sidewalk, making a grating noise.

Sarah didn't seem to notice her... but Chris did. He saw how the other pedestrians reacted to her, how they, perhaps sensing something odd in her creaking bones, gave her a slightly wider berth.

How she made the air around her like a frigid vacuum... how she tilted her head back and inhaled in spurts—air whistling through the jet-black forest of her nose hairs, how she went... *AHHH... AHHH... AHHH-CHOOOOOO!!!* kicking her head forward, sneezing directly into Sarah's mouth.

Sarah's head had jerked back—receiving it.

Phlegm and spit and whatever disease the crone carried traveled within globules of sick-wetness that now slicked the insides of Sarah's cheeks.

Sarah held her face. Her mouth. Her throat. Her lips. And Chris held her.

She started to wail, and to sob, and the very old woman smiled from ear to ear and began hustling away—much faster than she'd ever been before.

Chris rubbed his wife's back and shoulders, shushed and coddled her, telling her it was going to be ok. But it didn't work—she kept crying. And he had no plan of action.

Should he call the police? Should he confront the sick old lady? Publicly shame her, maybe?

He peered everywhere in pursuit of the hag, but she was gone. Having swiftly disappeared into the crowd. Passersby stopped and ogled wide-eyed while Sarah trembled.

She then began to wretch... her stomach heaving as her esophagus constricted... while the elderly woman's snot bumpily slid down her throat like beads of rice glommed together with a raw egg. It was terrible. She bawled and whimpered... but she didn't end up vomiting.

"It's ok, honey, it's ok. Come on," said Chris. "Let's go home."

He wrapped his arm around Sarah. They started the awful trudge to their Toyota Tacoma.

THE FOLLOWING weeks were plagued by imaginings of the vile crone. The pair tried their very best to forget her disgusting sneeze, but it proved a nearly unfathomable task, especially for Sarah.

The stranger's riveted witch-like-face being hard to forget.

Sarah cried a lot that first week. The experience having shaken her to the pit of her being. And she wasn't sure why.

But with time, all things ameliorate. Humans often forget their worst experiences, they move on. Filing awful memories away to the unvisited swaths of the unconscious mind where one's waking attention dare not look.

Chris and Sarah began having sex again, regularly. And a month after the sneezing incident, Sarah got pregnant. It was a surprise for both of them, since the doctors had said it was impossible.

But she had already begun showing signs: a small paunch forming on her usually slender body. It was unusual to show so early, but neither of the two cared much about what was *usual* and what wasn't. Chris touched his wife's stomach, rubbing a proud parental hand in warm arcs.

"This is incredible," he said. "Incredible! I can't believe it. I really can't believe it!"

Sarah looked at her husband, beaming as they lay in bed canoodling one another.

"It's real, unless it's from all the ice cream. But I really don't think it is."

Chris was elated. He'd never felt such joy. Such love imbuing his whole spirit. Chris the father. Chris the caretaker. His mind rolled on a billowy dreamscape of possibility.

He imagined presenting his toddling son with his old train set, complete with cowboys and Indians and brigands of the Wild West. He imagined taking him to tee-ball, rooting little Chris Jr. on from the blue-bricked dugout. He would have to be the coach, of course.

But what if he was to have a daughter? Would he give her his deceased sister's child-sized tiara and gown, so she could pretend to be Disney's Princess Aurora? Was he getting ahead of himself?

He'd have to protect her from boys... that much was certain. Probably have to chaperone her school dances, too. Answer the door, baring fangs between intermittent growls, warding off any potential suitors. Sounded like a lot of work. He looked into Sarah's soft brown eyes.

He hoped it was a boy. But either way, it was a miracle, really.

"I'm so happy," he told his wife.

Sarah smiled. "I am too."

"So, you've not had your period and it's been five weeks you say?" the OB-GYN asked. His name was Doctor Holman.

Holman had a five o'clock shadow and a mop of unruly gray hair. His head swooped on a sagging neck—so his apathetic eyes could surveil the room.

He sported a crumpled doctor's coat and under it, crumpled scrubs. His teeth were stained a flypaper yellow from a lifetime of coffee and cigarettes. The whole appearance, when taken together, reeked of depression. His breath reeked, too.

His office, on the other hand, was ivory-hued—the walls, the desks, the papers, the receptionist's teeth, everything. The whole place was matter-of-fact. Antiseptic. Synthetic. Sterile.

"No. It was supposed to come two weeks ago... then nothing," said Sarah. "I thought we should come in, because, you know, I'm showing, or at least we think I am."

Chris nodded behind his wife. He felt like he had to back her up, even though anyone could see the baby bump forming.

"Hmmm." Holman contorted his face. "Have you been having stomach pains of any kind? Anything out of the ordinary? Morning sickness, anything like that?"

"Well," Sarah looked to her husband.

"She has felt a little uncomfortable every once in a while, but that's normal, right?" said Chris.

"Yes, very normal if she's pregnant. But also normal for a tumor. Can I get you to lie back?"

"What!?" Chris yelped.

"It's ok, honey," Sarah outstretched her hand to grab Chris's forearm. "He's right, it could be anything. They used to say I was barren, ha-ha."

Sarah looked worried. Her eyes were big and watery like uncooked eggs. Chris clenched his fists at his sides. Not only did Holman not laugh at his wife's joke, he coolly said her baby bump could be a tumor. *Who the hell does that?*

The room was becoming uncomfortable.

Holman lifted Sarah's shirt and squirted a large amount of propylene glycol on her first-trimester paunch. The gel was frigid, Sarah hissed through her teeth.

"We're going to do an ultrasound, get to the bottom of this baby situation," said Holman. He was a strange man, the sort of medical professional that seems lost in his own world, like the patients he's diagnosing aren't even present.

Holman glided the probing instrument across Sarah's stomach. Sarah wrung Chris's hand, eyes darting from the cold doctor with his cold gel to the monitor where a nascent human should be forming. Chris had his eyes closed, hoping.

Thump, Thump, Thump...

"Ah, a heartbeat," said Holman.

Sarah and Chris cheered. They hugged. They embraced. You'd have thought they'd won the World Series. Doctor Holman peered at them... then at the monitor on his left.

He seemed befuddled. Let down even.

"Seems you aren't so *infertile* after all," he said. His voice resonated bitter through the lily-white room. These words were hard for him to speak, due to some hang-up or past trauma of his own. He didn't like seeing people happy.

"Congratulations Mrs. Mitchell. Remember to schedule your next appointment with the front desk, and leave us a good review online."

The OB-GYN marched his way through the room—his coat almost flapping behind him. He was fuming, and Chris wasn't exactly sure why. He cantankerously passed through the door, then was gone, but the couple barely noticed.

Chris wiped the semi transparent gel from his wife's stomach in between embraces. They both cried.

Sarah changed her diet. She was to eat only the freshest of foods: lean meats, pasteurized dairy, dark and leafy greens, baked vegetables (easier to digest), and up to twelve ounces of fish a week, since more could be potentially harmful due to all the mercury (salmon not included, the healthy omega-3 fatty acids were useful at a time like this).

Sarah liked her salmon baked in the oven without the skin.

The glimmering grey-green scales reminded her that the fish was once a living organism, which made her queasy. It was a pain to peel it off the skin from the filet, but Chris obliged and never complained. He loved his wife and his unborn baby (which he hoped was a boy).

By the second month, Sarah's womb had expanded even more and she began wearing baggy sweaters, cotton maternity shirts, and Chris's old high school hockey jerseys around the house

Today, she shuffled from their bedroom white as a sheet— swarthy crescents under her eyes, in a white tall-tee that draped down just above her girlish knees.

Usually an early riser, Sarah had become accustomed to waking later and later in the day. It was now noon. At first, Chris didn't see her. He was scanning some potential ads for his marketing firm, which sold slogans, cheery images, and commercials to a myriad of companies.

"Try on a new helmet," one of the advertisements said. "It's the only way to keep your head in the game."

Awful. Chris gently rapped at his forehead with his knuckles, as though it were a door which would be answered by a better, more marketable idea.

His current client was a sporting goods store in Alexandria: LENNY HUGGINS' LEAPING LOGISTICS. But he had had a huge mental block as of late, with the baby coming and all.

He kneaded the folds at the bridge of his nose between his tired fingers; then rolled his thumbs through the thicket of his eyebrows. Sarah stood in the doorway of their shared bedroom, studiously watching him—eyes big like a bush baby's.

Chris heard the splatter before he ever saw his wife. Flicking his head around, he saw Sarah projectile spewing what looked to be cherry pie. Only it was thicker. And it was neon green.

Chris rushed to Sarah's side and placed his caregiving hands on her shoulders—looking around while whispering:

"It's ok. It's just fine. Just a little of the illness that comes with the pregnancy."

Sarah was trembling, her body bent at an acute angle.

Her husband snatched the plaid blanket that was bundled up at the foot of their sectional couch. He tossed it over Sarah's quivering shoulders, as though he were putting out a small fire. He then led Sarah to the same couch and helped her to sit.

She slunk back. Her face beaded with sweat. Eyes mashed together into frowning slits. Chris looked at his wife worried. Placing a hand on his wife's belly, he started perspiring, too. Sarah's stomach seemed to be *writhing*.

"S TEAKS . I WANT TO HAVE STEAKS ," Sarah told him.

She looked him in the eyes when she spoke, very sternly. He didn't know what to do or say. Red meat wasn't necessarily part of her meal plan. According to everything they'd read, it would make her nauseous.

"Ah, do you want them cooked well-done?"

Sarah shrugged, "Just get them today. Please!"

Sarah pivoted away from her husband—her distended globe of a stomach silhouetted against the light filtering in from the curtains. It had only been two and a half months.

Aside from her body (which seemed to be irregularly sweating), Sarah's mood had been shifting, too. She was ornery. Brooding.

Not her peaceful, bubbly self.

Sometimes, Chris would enter their bedroom and catch Sarah laying on her side in the bed, staring unblinkingly at the blank-eggshell white wall. He'd watch in horror as she laughed and chittered, stringing together odd syllables that made no real words.

Was she watching some movie on that wall that only she was welcomed to view? He didn't know, and he dared not ask *again*. The last time, she snarled at him and called him a pussy.

CHRIS SPRINTED from the bedroom that night. He'd had a dream where a goo-sopped hand caressed his cheek, then slowly slid down his chest. It felt so real. So uncomfortable. When he awoke, he just reacted. He just ran.

It wasn't until Chris was halfway down the street that he realized he was dreaming and began to slow down. He turned back, and began walking under the streetlamps, clearly shaken.

He rubbed his forehead with his clammy palm, trying to remember what'd just happened. Did he wake Sarah up during all of that? Good Lord! He hoped not.

"Man, I'm about to hear it," he thought to himself.

Chris was almost back to his front yard when he saw the blood. A little track of scarlet blots shimmered on the asphalt. They increased in size the further he walked until he saw it.

A small dog had been gutted and laid in their yard. He took a few steps back and rubbed his eyes. Milo. The neighbor's puggle. Torn into as if it were a rack of lamb. By what? The biggest predator around Northern Virginia is a fox. Coyotes are pretty rare.

Chris gawked at the dead animal, tracing entrails that snaked through his grass. A hissing, as though a nest of snakes was stirred. And then, the sprinklers cut on.

Sighing and spurting and the little dead dog—eyes petrified and black, still lay there, being drizzled, being baptized by the outside water. It was six am. Chris ran into his house, checked the fridge, and saw the steaks were also missing.

No pans had been used and the backyard grill coverlet was still firmly secured by a bungee cord. Sarah lay asleep on her back, sweating. Her enormous stomach heaving wavelike with her chest in the twilight.

"How COULD you think I ate the neighbor's dog!" Sarah was hysterical.

"You've been acting really weird lately! And your stomach, well, it's not supposed to be that big. Not yet!"

She looked at her husband, her soft brown eyes glistening in the kitchen. The same eyes he'd fallen in love with. The same eyes that seemed to *hurt* so much lately. She began to sob. Sliding her back down the wall, palming her face.

Chris ran to her, as he had so many other times. And he held her.

"I don't know what's going on with me..." she wept. "I feel so... so... different!"

"It's ok. I'll call Doctor Holman. We'll get this all sorted out."

Sarah nodded her beautiful, vulpine head. Up and down. Up and down.

"Thank you," she said. "I don't know what I'd do without you."

"DOCTOR HOLMAN IS AWAY for a few weeks. Would you like to schedule an appointment for when he returns?"

"No. No. I really need one now..."

"Is this an emergency? If so, please call 911."

"No, not an emergency. We're just really worried..."

"It's ok," Sarah whispered over her husband's shoulder. "Just schedule it for when he comes back. I'll be fine. I'm already feeling better."

"Fine, ah... yes we'll schedule it for when he's back in two weeks."

"Well, that week is booked. But I can schedule it for the week after."

"So, in three weeks!?"

"Sir, please control your tone with me. If you want to be disrespectful you can call somewhere else. And yes. In three weeks."

"Fine, ok. Three weeks then."

Chris tried to control his *tone* until the date was set and he could hang up the receiver. Finally, they finished setting the appointment.

He turned to Sarah, who smiled.

"Everything's going to be fine," he told her, stroking her cheek.

She nodded; her mind was somewhere else.

HE WOKE in the middle of the night. Sarah was thrashing, screaming. Flicking on all the lights, he ran to her. Held her down. Repeated her name over and over until she woke up.

He'd never seen her eyes like that. Still big and brown, but so very terrified.

"What's wrong? What's wrong!" he shouted.

"It's... it's..." Sarah lifted her cotton shirt, soaked with sweat.

A small hand was pushing up and out from inside her body, near her ribs, outside of her womb. It was moving, disappearing, and then reappearing under different swaths of flesh. Sarah screamed.

"I'll call 911!"

When the paramedics came, Sarah told them that everything was fine. She'd just had a nightmare. The ambulance crew seethed, understandably upset by the situation. They reprimanded Chris, who sat on the couch prattling to himself in disbelief.

NO MATTER how bad it got, something in Sarah wouldn't allow Chris to dial 911. Not again. She'd plead for him to call. Then he'd grab the receiver. And then she'd scream for him not to. Saying this was all normal. She'd be sweet... and then she'd call him a small-dicked fucking bastard son of a bitch.

Sarah never spoke like that before.

Chris watched in horror. Her skin was changing in very disgusting ways. Things squirmed internally, stressing the flesh of her thighs and ribcage and back.

Sometimes extra vertebrae (or some manifestation resembling extra vertebrae) jutted out, all knobby, next to Sarah's delicate spine. Sarah would convulse. Then they'd disappear.

Maybe she'd become stricken with some neurological disease, her nerve endings all wrestling, trying to find a comfortable position in her small body.

Chris could swear that he saw hands pushing out at the flesh from under Sarah's arms. She would scream. Her feminine face contorted in pain. It was too much.

"What do I do... what do we do..." she murmured.

"I have to take you to the hospital!"

"NO!" her voice bellowed. But it didn't sound like hers.

"I'll call a priest then!"

"NO!!" it bellowed again.

Then, suddenly, Sarah's small mouth uttered: "Just hold me... if you call them, I'm afraid they'll take our baby."

She cried often after these bouts. And so did he.

In a matter of days, Sarah's body had become deformed and contorted. Something was growing inside of her. And she was in much pain. Chris couldn't take it any longer, seeing this *thing* that was feasting on her insides—cracking her frame to suit its devilish will.

Was it still his baby in there? If so, it was the biggest damned baby he'd ever seen. And that baby, well, it was killing Sarah.

He watched his beloved slumped over in the living room, the arms and legs of the *thing* jockeying around on the inside, clambering, turning her bones into a jungle gym.

Against Sarah's wishes, Chris dialed Doctor Holman again. He'd done this multiple other times, always furtively. This time, he was hiding in the bathtub. And, after his emotional pleading, the call center lady patched him through to Doctor Holman's cell.

"Go for Holman," intoned a grumbly voice.

"Doctor Holman..."

"Yes?"

"This is Chris, Chris Mitchell. You saw my wife Sarah and I about a month ago. We really need your help."

"Who?"

"Mitchell! You said my wife's, or our baby, might be a tumor. I think you may have been right. Or something is very wrong! Please, can you come?"

There was silence on the other line, followed by a gravelly noise from the throat, and an inhaling noise—the sound it makes when somebody is sucking down the butt of a cigarette.

Holman proceeded to tell Chris that he thought his wife was infertile, so he was honestly taken aback by the whole thing. He, himself, had had a wife who suffered many miscarriages, their marriage then fell apart. He developed a serious need for alcohol.

Drank it in the shower. Put it in his coffee. Even tried to make some once. Bathtub hooch, he called it. Made him go blind in one eye and deaf in one ear.

When he'd seen Sarah, who was supposed to be barren, with a child—well, it reminded him of his own woes. He went on a bender. He lost his share of the office to his partner, a young up and comer OB-GYN by the name of Midge Montgomery.

Holman was clearly intoxicated. He slurred a lot during his rambling... his spilling of the beans. But he agreed to head straight over. And for this, Chris was thankful.

THE DRUNK DOCTOR arrived a few hours later. Despite his overall crummy appearance, his eyes showed genuine concern, and Chris was desperate. He escorted the OB-GYN into his house, offering to take his ashtray-smelling coat from him, but the doctor turned him down.

Holman looked around... his rheumy eyes searching until he saw, *her*. Sarah lay at a slight angle on the couch, her body writhed grotesque, gnarled, freakish in its contours.

Holman removed his spectacles, his mouth opened wide in awe, studying the scene. Before Chris could speak, the old sot was trundling toward Sarah. Sarah moaned on the couch as Holman sat down on the ottoman before her.

"What do we have here," Holman inquired. He lifted Sarah's shirt with a tentative hand, seeing the shifting nooks and ridges just below her flesh. She breathed in pain as he continued to study the human tectonics.

"This is unlike any baby I've ever seen..." Holman looked over his shoulder, worriedly.

Chris shoved his pointer knuckle in his mouth, an affectation he acquired to stifle tears.

"What in the world is this?" Holman continued prodding and poring over the warped flesh, inch by centimeter by inch, until he saw the hand—it pushed out from within, embossing itself on Sarah's wriggling side.

Holman recoiled. Steeling himself, he extended a shaky hand, pressing his finger to the smaller hand that lay within. It grabbed from beneath the skin. And it twisted. And it wrenched Holman's finger, breaking it many times over.

Holman yowled. His eyelids peeled back as spittle flew from his mouth.

Chris stayed put, his body suddenly feeling heavy with fear.

Holman turned, outstretching his arm, holding the mangled digits before his petrified gaze to assess the damage. He shot up from the ottoman.

"YOu NEed aN aMbuLANCE HErE, IMMEDIATELY! For HER and for ME!" The reality of the situation had finally reached the pit of his drunken mind.

Chris nodded in the affirmative.

Sarah muttered, "*No*."

Somehow, someway, she reared up behind the startled gynecologist, a childbearing monstrosity, wincing from the exertion. She was barely in control, yet she bowled Holman over and he landed with a crash through the wicker end table.

Chris froze. Stood. And watched.

Swiftly, he tread backwards, cowering meekly against the far wall as whatever possessed Sarah reached, flexing her skin to the utmost point before it would rip. It clutched Holman's throat.

The doctor seemed to want to say something. Instead, being throttled, tobacco-flavored spit bubbled at the corners of his mouth. His eyes, alarmed and horror-stricken, looked a lot like the mauled neighbor's dog, Milo, when all was said and done.

They were wide open. A glossy black, like crow feathers. And they were settled on Chris' eyes while Sarah crouched over him, wrenching the life from his body, turning his throat into a blood-spurting hollow that stained their new carpet.

Sarah cried out, her unwieldy frame ratcheting left and right, the *thing* within her skin gripping at a handful of gore. Sarah stumbled back. She fell on the couch. She panted.

THE BODY LAY there for a few hours. Frozen stiff with fear, Chris huddled in the kitchen. Sarah would moan and roll indolently from side to side on the couch, her shirt, now red, rippling as the thing inside her jostled.

There's no one I can call now, Chris thought. He scooted himself across the tile floor until he was hidden behind their kitchen counter.

"No one I can turn to. No one! My wife is a killer. No! Whatever is in her did this. They'd understand... NO... they wouldn't understand. They'd kill her and my baby... my baby... is *he* ok?"

It wasn't cold in the room, yet Chris's teeth clattered together like small billiard balls. He shook. He trembled.

My baby... my wife... Sarah. I have to help her. Only I can help her, now. But the body, Holman's body. I'll have to deal with it later. Does that make me an accomplice? Can't think like that, can't think like that. Have to help her. Have to get up.

Chris pressed his hands to the floor and slowly lifted himself until he was peeking over the kitchen counter. Sarah was half asleep, a macabre and gruesome sight. Her stomach, her side, her neck, her arms, and her legs squirmed. She moaned.

He went to her, stepping around the large lake of blood seeping from the OB-GYN's neck, until he stood before the couch. He grabbed the plaid blanket from beside Sarah and pivoted and tossed it over Holman's body—shrouding his dead dog eyes.

Swallowing back his fear, he crouched on one knee, put his hand forth, and gently took the twitching hand of his wife.

"It's going to be Ok," he told her. "Everything is fine."

Chris forced a smile. Sarah groaned.

"Let's get you in the shower. Let's get you all cleaned up. Ok?" Chris wasn't really asking. Slowly, carefully, he lifted Sarah to her feet. The *entity* within her seemed to be rolling around on itself, tying itself in a bow—he made careful to avoid its grasping hands, and he walked his wife to their bathroom.

Chris turned on the water, placed Sarah in the tub. And he washed her as if she were his baby. He scrubbed with a yellow-now-red loofah, under the arms, minding the deformed ridges and the roiling bedlam, scrubbing the stomach, the kicking legs, scrubbing the breasts, amorphous and misplaced, scrubbing, scrubbing, scrubbing, the caked blood away.

THEY LAY IN BED, just as they had done for an entire decade, beside one another. Chris mindfully positioned Sarah so her face looked in his direction—her beautiful, vulpine face. The face he loved. The face he vowed to always protect.

Her eyes were closed in a wincing, somnambulant state. His were wide open.

Chris had dressed her in her favorite pregnancy pajamas. Silk. From her favorite store, Ann Taylor Loft. She suddenly blinked and grimaced and the *thing* moved and gained invaluable ground within her.

Where Sarah's ear, temple, and rosy cheek should've been, on the side facing away from Chris, wriggled an immense growth. It was a second, hideous face, protruding from Sarah's.

A nose, cheekbones, and eyes could be seen stressing the skin. Sarah, his Sarah. Chris tried not to blink his eyes. He didn't want to forget her. Didn't want to forget what she looked like, and, for a moment... she looked at him.

She was scared, he could see it in her soft brown eyes. Pushing one hand out, he stroked the side of the cheek that was still hers.

"What's... happening... to... me..." she whispered.

"It's ok. It's ok," Chris whimpered. "Everything's going to be fine."

He was sobbing now, and so was Sarah. They hugged, as best they could and he told her he loved her. But she didn't respond, she was gone again, in her semiconscious state.

Chris didn't stop staring. Eyes trying to soak her all in, trying to remember her while she was still by his side.

He wanted to have something for the future, something that would care for him in his latter days. Not a child. But, her memory.

THE HOURS flitted by and by and all was still in the house, other than what jostled inside of Sarah's skin. The room was nearly noiseless, despite the air conditioning and a gurgling-sloshing sound and the creaking of bones.

A gentle predawn light began to streak through their bedroom curtains....Yet the bed, for the most part, remained ensconced in shadow.

Chris must have fallen asleep.

Something sat up in the bed beside him, and it stirred him awake. He could only see the silhouette, could only see the vague outline.

"*Sarah*," Chris's voice shook. He placed a shaky palm on her shoulder, feeling the border of a new hunch on her back.

Sarah turned and grinned with pale thin lips that curled up in the corners. Her nose was long and jagged; her eyes were beady vortices to frigid, unfeeling, nowhere; her face massively wrinkled.

It wasn't her.

"Thank you for having me," the crone said, *laughing, chortling, croaking*, staring at Chris as he screamed and fell from the bed.

The ragged woman, that one who had sneezed in Sarah's mouth months before, scooted herself off the bed and shambled to the doorway. She turned to look at Chris, curled against the wall, knuckles of his fist shoved into his mouth.

"You know you're supposed to say bless you when somebody sneezes." She smiled, wretchedly.

"Where is she, what have you done with my wife..."

The old woman glowered at Chris, then smiled again, and left— moving more swiftly than she ever had before, rushing with a renewed vigor.

She didn't shut the door behind her.

Chris remained there, curled up on the floor, rocking on his haunches for what seemed like an eternity. Until the police arrived.

MY FELINE FRIENDS

I wanted them to look like cats. Good thing women love dermal fillers as much as kitties love milk, so it worked out quite well.

I tend to tell them their smile is pulling from one side, causing significant "jowling" wherein we find the nasolabial folds. Nasolabial folds are smile lines. It's good to throw around such jargon, and spew nonsensical dross such as full-face sprinkle, neurotoxin obliterators, cannula, and myo-modulation, so my future felines will think I'm distinguished.

I tell them they're restoring volume to their cheeks, and that cheeks can be so powerful. "I don't want to change who you are. I only want to enhance your natural beauty. I want to bring you back to where you might've been five years ago," I say.

Of course, this is a lie. Like I said, I want them to look like cats.

BLYTHE WAS COMING in for her fourteenth Cybella treatment, which is an injector that permanently burns fat from the body, allegedly. I'd shot it under her chin, in her arm flab, on her back fat, and so on. And she comes in and says:

"Nurse Schetfy, you've been so instrumental in my personal transformation, which is why I'm scared now, maybe my defects can't be helped."

She is sitting on the table in my sterile, bright office, with her quinquagenarian feet swinging, and skin stretched and inflated from all of the Rejuvéderm Ultra Plus shots I'd given her.

Her lips have been pumped with large amounts of Glotox in the past month—it was supposed to detract from her long witchlike nose and reduce her "gummy smile." A gummy smile is when you have excessive gingival display when you smile, in other words, when you show too much of your gums when you grin. We've all seen it, small teeth, big gums, it's disgusting.

"Your defects can be helped, Blythe. You just have to trust me and we will solve this thing together."

"But nurse, where you gave me the Cybella injections, well LOOK!"

Blythe pulled her blouse up to expose her belly covered in fur.

"That's perfectly natural, sweetie, it's just your body producing estrogen because your beauty is coming to the surface."

"It is...?"

"Yes! Of course!" I clasped my hands reassuringly.

"Now, for today, what do you say about adding more volume to your cheeks, so they hold even firmer and really Glow!"

"But, Nurse Schefty, I've had so many injections in my cheeks, are you sure this is a good idea?"

"Yes, trust me, girl. I know what I'm doing."

She was a deformed atrocity—an atrocity that I feel very proud of creating. The cheeks in question were puffed out pin cushions perforated hundreds of times, right where the smile lines should've been.

I visualized whiskers jutting from those stiffened pink mounds, which made me very happy.

I laid my patient on her back while gently susurrating, "*Shhhh, shhhh, shhhh,*" like I used to do to my childhood feline, Binky, when I was a little girl.

I injected her cheeks with more Glotox and then had her open her mouth, picturing her incisors shrunken and her canines stretched like stalactites and stalagmites crisscrossing in a carnivorous sort of way.

"Those could shear a mouse," I whispered.

"What!?" Blythe said.

"Oh, uhm, nothing... please relax."

The needle slipped in and out of her skin while I dabbed at the fresh wounds. My heart fluttered, imagining the cat woman she was to become. When I lost my sweet Binky, after my mother told me she had "run away," I had never been so utterly lonely. It's a loneliness that still lasts.

Blythe was done with her injections. I hugged her and told her all would be "Ok, just trust in the beautification process," and ushered her out the door. I went to the waiting room to call upon my next client, and there they all were, staring up at me with their eyes like sapphire and jade, highlighting their intrinsic neediness of my attention.

Those eyes followed my every movement, as if I were a piece of yarn. I marveled at all the progress I'd made with their personal transformations. And I wondered if they would notice the odd pupils in the room, like almonds or slits, or if they would think it strange that some were sitting on inflatable donuts—I had been injecting growth hormones at the base of their spines in hopes of some sprouting tails.

They all started beckoning me, one after the other, asking if it was almost their turn.

"Nurse Schefty. Nurse Schefty. I have a five o'clock dinner with a client. I need to look perfect to close this deal. Please!"

"Nurse! Nurse! I need to pick my step-kids up from Saint Lawrence's in an hour. Can I go next so you can firm up my forehead?"

"I'll be with you all in a moment, ladies. Michelle, you're up now. How are you feeling my dear?"

"Not so well, Nurse Schefty. I'm glad you asked," she grinned, baring her teeth for all in the lobby to see.

"Well, girl," I said. "Must be time for your tweakment!"

Michelle rose from her seat, both splayfooted and tottering. I'd managed to increase the distance between her metatarsal bones, widening the forefront of her feet. In this way, she now maneuvered on her pads, much like cats do.

I said this odd way of walking would make men notice her ass. In actuality, it was just funny to look at. She returned a heavily creased People magazine to the coffee table and waddled in my direction.

The others pouted, sulking in their seats, and fiddling with their preposterous hairdos as I closed the door separating my world and theirs. I put my hand on the middle of Michelle's back. And I swear she purred, so I smiled.

I sat her on the little medical table in my office, then looked her over. Her eyes were a bright yellow, and her pupils flitted about. She jittered a little in the air conditioning, but when I asked if she was cold, she told me she wasn't. Nonetheless, I presented her with a small sweater that smelt of catnip.

Michelle had a lighthouse keeper's slur when she spoke since I had been injecting her tongue for the last four months.

I said broadening her tongue would morph the dimensions of her jawline since she thought her jawline was too weak. She thought the absence of a discernible jawbone, coupled with her long, svelte neck, made her look like a five-foot-five, brunette finger.

She was eager to get it fixed, so she could gallivant around town searching for a man naïve enough to be her husband. But I hadn't been widening her tongue at all or subsequently widening the bones on the sides of her face, as I had told her, and as she had believed.

"What exactly are you doing to me?" she slurred.

"Oh, honey. I'm just unleashing your natural beauty so the world can see! You know that! Now, tilt your head back, please."

She did.

"Now open your mouth..."

"Thank you. Stick out your tongue," and she did, and I got the syringe ready. Her tongue bristled with papillae, backward-facing spines containing keratin that cats use to rip the flesh from their prey. Oh, they were coming in so nicely.

"You may feel a pinch," I said, pushing the needle in and watching the little forest of spines grow as I did so. She goggled wide-eyed and befuddled—a single tear running from her eye. Oh, my little Mee-Chee.

"You know this is not standard practice, so please, keep it between us," I said, brushing the hair back from her triangularly cropped ear.

"I know, I know," Michelle slurred. "I just want to be beautiful, Nurse Schefty."

"And you are! Just never leave my side!" I said. "Popsicle, sweetie?"

"Um, Ok..."

I snatched a bar of frozen milk from my freezer, then shoved it in her hand. She took it, gladly. "Have you been taking the medication I prescribed?" I asked.

"Yes," she said. "But it's hard to see, except at night, sometimes."

"Oh! Don't worry, that's a normal part of the process! Just try to avoid vacuuming and water. Might fray the nerves."

Michelle made a face as she tasted the popsicle. I went on.

"Can you do that for me, sweetie? Also, remember to eat lots of tuna sashimi and beef tartar, it's good for the glutes... will make them pop."

"Ok..." she said. I escorted her from my office and watched her lope ahead of me. Her transmutation was bestial, yet she was so eager for beauty she trusted in my practice. And I, in return, was gaining what I hoped would be a lifelong companion.

I hugged her before we reached the waiting room, and she seemed to purr again. I smiled. And she went out the door as I stepped into the antechamber. Within, the women glowered collectively, narrowing their almond-shaped pupils into vertical black dashes.

They called out restlessly, jockeying for "Nurse Schefty!" as their desperation saturated the room. One of the women, Amy Decamp, grabbed at my wrist. Her grip seemed mighty strong for such a slim priss, and she pulled at me with a disconsolate look on her wrinkle-less face.

"Nurse, Nurse, please, I really need your help. I noticed the beginnings of crow's feet the other day and I've been absolutely hysterical."

"Don't listen to her! I was first!" screamed another patient of mine, named Abilene. "You promised to increase my Rejuvéderm injections before New Years!"

"Ladies, ladies, you will all have your turn. Now, please, just try your best to remain calm."

They wriggled in their seats and rubbed their arms against their hips, muttering. So, I told my receptionist to bring them a snack while they waited... and soon, they were presented with a platter of sliced cheese. Cats love cheese.

These women really needed me, and in their absolute neediness, I didn't feel so alone. I was the remedy to all of their mental hurt. As they were mine. As I stood there, surrounded by my crying cats, I felt comforted.

"Next up, is Lizzy," I said, and the other women groaned.

"How are you today, Lizzy, my dear?"

She strode to me like a proud tabby cat, all mottled, sashaying as if she owned the place. Her wide countenance was glistening under the lobby's fluorescent fixtures.

"Good, good, I think," she glanced at her gilded watch. "Can we make it quick? I don't want to get stuck in traffic."

"Sure thing, sweetums," I said, placing a hand on her shoulder. She recoiled at the touch, arching her back as though she were upset with me.

"Is everything ok?" I asked.

"Yes. You just left me waiting for so long. Let's go. Please."

I nodded, coyly. She was an outdoor cat, that much was certain. Unbroken and unbridled; untamed and feral. I loved every moment with her.

I brought her to my office—presenting her with multiple Rejuvéderm injections that were, in actuality, serums infused with steroids and feline DNA. I injected three into the base of her spine, which was furry, I might add. And she hissed, wildly blowing off steam.

Next, I stabbed at her ballooning lips and poked at her massive jowls over and over again with my needle, erasing what was left of her humanity, until her next "tweakment," of course. She blinked at me, just an anthropomorphic cat with a harsh attitude.

"Are we done here?" she asked. "I have a Soul Cycle class to get to..."

"Oh, be careful, sweetie. Wouldn't want to mess up those nails of yours..."

Her face didn't move, it wasn't able to. Yet her deep green eyes said all there was to say. Lizzy was fuming. She snorted at me. So, I tried to calm her down.

"Everything's ok, my sweet, sweet, Whiskers."

"What'd you call me!?"

"Oh, nothing," I responded quickly and took her hand, studying the expertly sharpened claws surmounting her slender, lightly furred fingers.

"Let me go!" she pulled her hand away and I stumbled forward, stunned.

She seemed even more disgruntled than before—some mutation fraught with a googol of emotions at once. I let her go, my angry kitty. She abruptly pivoted and made her way out of my office.

I followed, leaving a safe distance, making my way back to the lobby.

I was upset by our interaction, but I knew women, as well as cats, get testy sometimes. I watched Lizzy storm out of the building, and I saw that all of the other women were too preoccupied with their personal needs of appearance alteration that they didn't seem to notice.

As I entered the waiting room, once again, my litter of patients was rowdier than ever. They were shouting now, and I could see that the cheese tray had been overturned, and that my receptionist had locked herself away.

"NURSE! NURSE!" they were screaming all at once.

They began standing and shoving at each other, corralling me into the center of the room, invading my space.

"Is it my turn yet? I've been waiting for almost two hours!" said a bushy-haired woman, who looked like a Maine Coon, with her bloated face unmoving.

"No! It's my turn! I'm up now!!" said the woman who'd grabbed my wrist earlier.

"You bitch! I said stop elbowing me!" hollered one of my favorite patients, Elise, brandishing her sharp fangs. The weird thing was, she seemed to be elbowing the others.

My patients closed in and in and in on me, constricting their circle. And as they screamed, their hollering for infinite Glotox injections intermingled, molesting my eardrums with their shrillness.

I reeled, realizing their voices were no longer befitting of humanity. In fact, they were not screaming at all.

My patients were *meowing*. Awful, hurting, frantic, mews. But for a short, fading moment, I didn't feel so utterly alone. I was flanked on every side by my companions. These ladies were my pets. They were my cats, my milk-licking replacements.

They needed me to care for them, more than Binky ever had.

One of the women, Linda Mahoney, suddenly swiped at me with her claw, tearing the sleeve of my shirt and drawing blood. Another clutched at my hair, yoking my head backward, causing me to fall to the ground. I couldn't help but laugh at the irony of it all.

Looking up, I saw nothing but swollen, catlike faces. They were focusing in on me, as their fangs and pearlescent eyes glimmered violently in the lobby. I felt claws raking against my throat, sharpened teeth sinking into my cheeks and legs and arms, numerous paws slicing my belly crosswise, pulling at my innards.

I smiled crookedly, not alone, but enveloped in a writhing pile of my cat ladies, bleeding out on the lobby floor.

NIGHTWATCH

I heard something, or someone, rifling around in our trash cans again. It's not unusual. It's been going on for weeks. Always in the middle of the night, or early in the morning, depending on how you look at it. It's never at midnight.

Usually begins a few hours before dawn.

I go out there, as I have so many times, in my pajamas, with my flashlight, trying to catch the culprit. I see nothing. My garbage is strewn about my yard like the entrails of some combusted dump truck.

"Must be huge racoons," I quip to my pregnant wife, who chuckles softly, then rolls to her other side.

The next day, I decide to stake out my garbage cans, to catch the ne'er-do-well in the act. That night, I hide behind some hydrangea bushes, with a broom, and a flashlight, of course. It's not much of a plan. But shit, it's something.

And I see someone.

It's a man, I believe, due to the wide-set shoulders, the short hair, and the awkward gait. He or she is shuffling coltishly, zigzagging, dragging their slippers across the pavement. I hear a strange *skreeet* noise. Is the sound coming from his mouth, or his dragging feet... I can't pinpoint the source.

Maybe the person is on drugs, who knows, meandering under the streetlamps: illumined; then disappearing; lighted yet again; then vanishing; coalescing with the shadows.

The moon seems tremendous tonight. Like the night sky was made just for it. It's somehow comforting, that off-yellow lunar-satellite. Makes me feel a little like I'm not alone. I notice the stranger, a few feet now from my trash, looking back and forth, surveying, I assume, for adversaries.

I can clearly see now that it's a man. And he's off. The figure dives headlong into my garbage, pawing ravenously, throwing detritus around like a starved wildcat. I wait for a few breaths, mentally rehearsing my lines, "Hey you! Stop that!" No, that sounds weak. "Hey asshole! Remember me!?" No, that doesn't make much sense. I've never met him before, I assume.

I decide to go with... "Hey, jerk! Cut that out!"

I jump up and start rushing toward the fiend. I'm shining and shaking my flashlight at him, trying to unveil the madman's identity, trying to make him pay for his criminality, his "petty" crimes. He jerks his head back with such force I thought it'd rip from his shoulders. Startled. His eyes are as big as the moon and just as yellow.

Unshaven, bedraggled, willowy, with a tuffet of hair on an otherwise bare head. My foofaraw disturbs him, and he turns to run, but one of his slippers falls off. He stumbles to the ground awkwardly. I alight upon him like the holy wrath of the Old Testament.

"WHAT THE HELL DO YOU WANT WITH MY GARBAGE!" I holler.

He winces, so familiar it's strange. Familial almost. I can't bring myself to strike the bizarre man, as I'm not violent, much of this was just for show.

"WHO ARE YOU!?" I scream.

"I-uh... I'm your son..." the man says.

Stunned by his answer, and thinking he's definitely on drugs now, I respond logically, "Impossible, I don't have any kids. Except for the one that's on the way, if that counts."

"Yes... the unborn baby, Charles, that's me," he says.

Something about his voice is comforting. I feel my weird rage diminish while glaring into his jaundiced eyes. I help the stranger to his feet and notice he's not wearing slippers. They're sneakers that seem to be melting from overuse.

"So. What brings you here, son?" I say sarcastically, playing along.

"I come from the future. A man, by the name of Trembler, has built a time machine to the past."

"A time machine?"

"Yes. I wasn't supposed to go. But there was nobody else around. You see, the world was overrun by hyper-sentient automatons.

Everyone is dead. Well, pretty much everyone. I was surviving off garbage, and he sent me back here, to alter earth's timeline."

"You? You're not very impressive. Pardon my bluntness."

"Like I said, I was the only choice. He had to stay to keep the portal open in case he could send others back. He said, though, that I'm most likely humanity's last and only hope."

"And you're going to stop these automatons by eating your, I'm assuming dead, parents' garbage?"

"I was keeping my strength up until I thought of a plan. But I think I've got it now."

"Yea, what's that?"

"You still work at Ultra-technic Labs? Developing AI pantsuits and ties and bifocals?"

"Yeah... What are you getting at? You could've just found that on my tax forms."

Before the stranger could answer, a shrill-screech echoed from between the homes of our suburban neighborhood. It, to say the least, stifled the conversation. Without warning, almost immediately, my cul-de-sac was swarmed with police cruisers.

Blue and red lights spilling into the street; transposing darkness with a bath of gleam; transmuting night into bicolored day.

The officers rushed from their cruisers and tackled the garbage eater.

"Wait!" I said, holding out my hand.

"Step back, sir. We'll handle it from here. You have nothing to worry about."

The stranger looked into my eyes, as they slammed him into the hood of the cop car. He seemed to be crying, and, future or not, he seemed to have traveled a long distance. The cops sped off, the cul-de-sac was soon vacant, as if I'd imagined the whole thing.

Inside, my wife's belly looked set to burst. She was sitting in our living room, basking under a lamp. She said she saw me wrestling with the bum, then she called the police. I sighed, confusedly. She smiled a grin so big it seemed her face was meant only for it.

"In unrelated news, I've thought of a name for our baby!"

"You did?"

"Charles!"

"Charles?"

"Yep! Came to me all of the sudden, when I saw you wrestling with that man... so strange..."

THE CEMETERY

He looked like a dehydrated salamander marooned under a heat lamp. His few remaining hairs, which were still jet-black, were slipping off the back of his head like greased up noodles on a linoleum floor.

"Do you need help with your bags, sir?" bellhops questioned when he was making the rounds on unimportant business trips.

"My bags? No, I don't think so, unless you mean the ones under my eyes!" he'd laugh, then add: "I'm exhausted!"

He couldn't remember how many times he'd used this joke. He did remember the first time he thought of it though, and that memory always came with a smile.

Erik Adler II was an economy unto himself and that was his downfall. He worked himself quite literally to death.

Unseen by his assistant for a week and a half, he was found slumped over his writing table with a Montblanc in his hand—bluish, pale, and rigid.

A stack of unsigned papers loomed in front of his corpse, blocking her view of him from the office door window. She'd thought he was out of town.

One fateful day she entered his office looking for a stapler. Cynthia shrieked and fainted. It would be another hour before she woke up and another hour and a half still until the medics arrived.

His obituary that weekend read:

Erik Adler II, war hero, loving father and husband leaves behind five children and seventeen grandchildren.

He is gone but never forgotten.

SEEING him lowered into the ground was the most difficult part for all of us. This man, who had been so energetic and purposeful his entire existence, was now some worm's dinner.

"At least Saint Peter will finally get help with his paperwork," quipped my sister, Aimee, trying to lighten the mood at his burial.

I didn't laugh.

THIS MORNING MARKS the anniversary of my grandfather's death. We are going to visit his gravestone. My mother, my sister and I all pile into our modern-day jalopy. The car creaks under our collective weight.

The mismatched hubcaps, one gun-metal gray, one rusty beige and two black, are nearly hidden under the chipped body of the tired sedan. The road usually seems bumpy, speckled with numerous potholes, but today it flows under our worn tires with an effortless ease.

Outside of the car windows, the trees and bushes expose their fresh foliage like some exhibit in Mother Nature's art gallery. Maybe the walnut-colored squirrels and the grey birds flittering about them are the museum's curators, chittering their odd facts.

We drive further and the trees disappear from sight. Soon, a cousin of the previous oak or evergreen materializes, reminding me that nothing is ever truly gone, it just takes a slightly different shape.

Time flies by, melting into infinity, as it always does.

We drive through the impressive iron gates of the graveyard, tall and wiry reminders of a gothic past that is always lurking some-where in the shadows. The car, which seems keen to be buried here, rattles to a stop on one of the roads that twist through the cemetery.

Stepping out, I walk on the dew capped grass of the graveyard, listening as earth squishes under my sneakers. Then, like some kind of a shockwave, the cemetery's hallowed, eternal silence comes, swallowing up the sound of my squelching steps.

A chill runs through me.

There's a strange loneliness about the landscape, which is ironic since so many people are buried here. The tombstones stick out from the ground like miniature buildings. Some of the more dilapidated plots go back as far as the 1800s. How different life must have been for the people of those eras.

Whole generations came and went and my parents hadn't even met each other at their neighborhood mixer. Something within me withered, feeling small and humbled by the epiphany: I'm just a speck of fleeting physicality, riding a wave of forever.

Yep, people had dreams and aspirations and loved ones and now they were mere dust. I read an old crumbling gravestone. The name written was for a Susan Merchant 1835-1877. The fading words are a shock to my nervous system:

"To Susan Merchant our beloved mother and grandmother we say: Sleep in, dear mother, thy work is done. Your mortal pang is past. Jesus has come and borne thee home, beyond the stormy blast."

I feel some ghostly presence descend on me while studying the epitaph. I picture a woman with a spotted apron on. She's smirking and clanging a dinner bell. Her children are being called indoors to enjoy an early supper. Steam rises from warm bowls of oatmeal. I can almost smell it. Then she turns to me, within my daydream, and says... "Thanks for stopping by."

As if someone had snapped their fingers, the hallucination crumbles in an instant and I'm back in the cemetery, eyes wide, like I had just met a ghost. With chills running through my whole body, I hurry away.

My sister and mom had left me behind to be with my thoughts. Now they're up a hill, just a few stone throws ahead.

As I'm running, I wonder if what I'd just experienced was real, or if I was going crazy. If I wasn't halfway to the insane asylum, Susan Merchant did seem thrilled to be remembered, even if it was only for an instant.

Eventually, wheezing in air, I sidle up to my mother and sister. We keep placing our feet on the grass, one in front of the other, reenacting a funeral procession.

Moving onward, ploddingly.

"There are so many dead people in the world. When do you think they'll have to start burying people vertically... instead of horizontally... you know, to save space?" Aimee asks.

Even though it's a decent joke, I don't want to encourage her too much so I only give her a half smile.

"You know, if you find a shovel, I bet you can find a really good suit for prom!" she whispers to me.

My half smile becomes a full one, then I shush her, and we keep walking.

I'M STANDING before the burial plot of my deceased grandpa. I share his name: Erik. I feel weird just thinking about it. We're not alike. He was much better than I am or will ever be. I get the feeling he's been buried there just as long as Susan Merchant. I know it's not true by over a century. Plus, his tombstone is still new looking, with crisp edges that glint under the sun, and freshly chiseled words.

I look over to see my mom whimpering, her chin, being down pulled by sorrow, bobs on her chest. I look at my feet, not knowing what to do.

"What in the hell is that?" my sister blurts out, nudging me in the ribs with her pointy elbow.

I glance up the hill, following her finger.

"I don't see anything, what?"

"Right there! Look!"

Then I see it. There is something crawling around on the top of the small hill. It's silhouetted in the sun and I can barely make out what it is.

"What is that? A wounded raccoon?" I ask.

"Please show some respect for your grandfather!" My mom is pissed. "If you can't be silent and reflect for a few minutes just go up there and see what it is! Or tell the groundskeeper. But don't make a commotion here! Not here! No, not here!"

Her voice is suffused with a deep sadness. The loss of her father still hurts her. It's why she's been drinking so much recently, I think. My mom turns her wetted cheeks from us, then fixes her gaze once more on the unmoving tomb.

"Let's leave her alone for a little while and check that out," I say to my sister.

Her face broadens from side-to-side with a deranged smirk. A transformation has taken place. My sister is now an albino jack-o'-lantern, the embodiment of childhood curiosity, even though she's in her mid-twenties.

We get closer and closer to the creature. I call it a creature now because it's unidentified. For all I know, it could be a tumbleweed or a soccer ball. It could be a half empty beer can, filled with a bunch of inebriated crickets. It could be some foreign government's all-terrain land droid, or maybe my first guess was right, and it is a wounded raccoon. What it actually is, was completely unexpected. We are both staring... at an infant.... a baby.

Our mouths drop open.

"Is that a baby?" I ask my sister, dumbfounded. I'm surveying the grounds for any sign of grief-stricken parents. I see no one.

"It is, it looks like Maggie from The Simpsons... Look, it's even going gaga." Aimee is pointing at the newborn. She seems to think her finger is a magic wand that can somehow make it disappear.

"What should we do?" she asks me.

"I don't know…"

"Maybe it has a nametag and a number to call in case it gets lost," she jokes.

"Shut up… I'm thinking… Did you see anyone earlier when we got here, or did you see a groundskeeper?"

"By groundskeeper, do you mean an old creepy guy holding a shovel, wearing overalls with no undergarments, while smelling like cheap scotch and rotting corpses? No, I haven't seen one." Aimee laughs nervously.

My sister has the annoying habit of joking in the few situations where she should be serious. I turn around, looking frantically for some clue of the baby's origin. Surprised, I see another bundle of joy crawling among the headstones nearby.

"Look!" My sister is pointing again and once more I follow her crooked finger, forgetting the second baby.

There is yet another, small and cuddly stranger. This one is sitting on top of a gravestone, swaying small feet back and forth. Rushing forward, I scoop up the infant, scared it might fall off the grave. I put him or her on the grass and pat the newborn once on the head.

"Look!" My sister yells again and I reel around.

Three more babies are crawling from behind a giant oak, shadowing the remains of the dead.

"What in the name of all that's normal?" I say as I continue to look around. I notice that there are babies appearing everywhere. In a few short minutes, the cemetery grounds are almost full. Drooling heaps of diaper-less dwarves are rolling around and piling up on one another.

"What do we do?" my sister screams to me. Babies are congregating at her feet.

"I don't know" I scream back amongst the throng of little, crawling people.

"Mom, are you ok?" I shout.

I'm looking down the hill to where my mom was. I see her trembling on top of grandpa's tombstone. Her knees are pulled tight against her chest. Her wide, frightened and saucer-like eyes seem to take up most of her face.

"What is this?" she screams.

"I don't know, just keep calm... they can't hurt you. They're just babies." I say, trying to calm her nerves.

"Look, they're all leaving!" my sister shouts.

I look toward the impressive black gates of the Cemetery. I see the crowd of babies making a mass migration, crawling out of the grave-yard in unison. It's a bizarre sight. Cars screech to a halt in the middle of the bustling street. Travelers exit their vehicles and people commence snapping photos on their phones, murmuring amongst themselves, going live on their social medias, not quite under-standing what they're seeing.

We run to my mother and we all huddle around each other, hugging and trying to make sense of what just happened. I see a newborn with a lick of jet-black hair cooing and shuffling from behind grandpa's tombstone.

"Dad!?" my mother gasps.

EL PERDIDO

The filthy outlaw was dehydrated, emaciated, and partly incapacitated. He trod along trail-less nature, coughing and slouching over the back of his two-tone speckled bronco whose name was Steve.

He spotted a village on the horizon, festooned with worn out establishments of moldering old Mexican style architecture.

A dirt-beige clocktower loomed in the distance, ironically crumbling from the time it told. This would have to do, he reckoned, at least the law wouldn't find him here. Hell, he didn't even know where here was.

The outlaw dug his heels into the horse, who, mind you, was just as tired as he was. And they tread past cacti and sun-bleached skeletons, while little lizards flicked their tongues skyward before scuttling away.

Soon, they were flanked by dilapidated buildings, stucco-white-things, seemingly abandoned. He tried to whistle, but his throat was too dry, his lips were too cracked, besieged by the heat and the unrelenting arid wind that seemed the breath of giants. The outlaw stabbed his spurs once again into Steve's flanks. The steed whinnied, tiredly, in what was more of a gargling wheeze than the cry of a healthy stallion.

The outlaw, Jan Schinke, scanned the buildings for any sign of life. All was quiet, save the howling wind and the broken-timbered blinds smacking the sides of the tired-out edifices, their only response to the timeless breeze of attrition.

Eyes, a few pairs at first, then a few more, then a couple more, materialized from the void. Soon there were scores of them. Gawking, disembodied, with crimson irises. They peered out of pitch-black windows, door frames, and attics.

"Hello," the outlaw whispered.

"*Quién eres tú?*" a voice hissed.

"No hablo," the outlaw mumbled.

"He said, who are you? What do you want?" This voice snarled and barked and howled simultaneously. It had the timbre of a great beast singing falsetto.

"My name is Jan, Jan Schinke, I just need a place to rest...." the outlaw abruptly fell off his horse. He was unconscious and lay limp and coiled like an atrophying snake.

When Jan awoke the next morning, he was lying in a strange bed. And his gunshot wounds had been wrapped with ointment-soaked linens. He'd been tended to. Save for a splitting headache, he felt quite alright.

Schinke was convalescing now, that much was for certain. *Where the fuck am I?* he wondered. The outlaw searched for his pistol. It wasn't on his waist. Then he saw it.

There, on the caked-in-dust nightstand beside him, was his revolver, sheathed in its worn-leather holster. Now he knew things were afoot, strange as all hell, and as eerie as Old Mother Hubbard could've squawked in her cupboard. He checked to see if his kidneys were still with him. They were.

He put on his shirt. It'd been neatly folded and placed next to the gun, by his unknown caretaker. Schinke buttoned it slowly, minding the pain in the side of his abdomen, his shoulder, his lance-punctured thigh. He also had a blown off thumb, of which remained only a jutting crag of calcium.

This too, was bandaged in his sleep. He moved very slowly.

And suddenly, Schinke's ears pricked up as an enchanting melody wafted from below the bedroom door. He shuffled to the habitation's window, floorboards creaking under newly cobbled boots.

Who the hell cobbled his boots?

He glanced out, furtive like a man in the throes of battle, used to situations where bullets whizzed by aimlessly, taking lives by chance occurrence. Only there were no bullets this time, and he was much relieved to see Steve fastened to a wooden handrail outside. He limped to the bedroom door, opened it, and ploddingly made his way out.

He was in what he now assumed to be, a brothel or a saloon of some kind. Schinke edged his way down the serpentine staircase, moving like an elderly and distinguished old man. The bar was completely vacuous, tables stood unused, stools un-sat-in, and there was no barkeep in sight.

The music continued though, ceaselessly, and for no one in particular. Schinke made eyes with the steam organ wherein the melody came. Then, bit by crimson skinned bit, he saw the figure playing the calliope.

It was a small demon, about three feet tall, ambiguous in gender, with a distended stomach and a barren-bald head. The creature grinned, enraptured with its tune. Its sharpened fangs glistened in the foyer of the sunlit bar. The thing didn't look up.

Schinke ambled past the demoniacal keyboard player, nude, but clothed with the palpable fear it created. He pushed open the swinging door to the saloon. But Steve, his horse, was gone. Schinke was confused and thought himself hallucinating.

He limped on into the town, seeing more little red bodiless eyes peering out at him from the spacious windows. He walked towards the edge of the settlement, which was but a few hundred yards away.

Somehow, the village's outskirts kept receding as he advanced. He stepped and stepped. The pueblo stretched and stretched, forever farther, bending over the weltering horizon.

He walked in this way for long, frustrating hours. Getting nowhere, his exit forever elusive. The demon's awful calliope rang out, omnipresent, echoing from every ramshackle edifice and sun-melting hovel. Soon, he collapsed. And when he awoke.... he was once again in the bed.

The music continued, much louder now, and the room sweltered hotter.

Sweat leaked from every orifice while his back ached and his mind became submerged in ubiquitous confusion. He heard Steve whinny, and he made his way to the window again. The horse was there. So, he exited the room. Completed the same routine, ignoring the little red devil, skirting past it, trying his best to find his steed who had somehow, once again, vanished.

Schinke ambled in perpetuity. His knees began to wobble, worn down from his bowlegged gait, and soon his knees buckled. The sand felt like blue flame to the touch. Schinke moaned and groveled, inching his way to some shade cast by the awning of an abandoned barber shop.

The porch of the shop was covered in what Schinke assumed were lingering hairs, shorn forever ago, but when he reached his destination, he found that the hairs were actually tiny snakes, the size of very thin worms. And they bit. And he screamed and slowly made his way back from whence he came.

Months passed monotonous and terrible, with the room ever-increasing in heat, and its paint oozing in streams off the diabolical partitions. The stallion always, forever, disappearing. He tried to shoot the demon, but the hilt on his pistol would become brazenly hot, causing the skin of his palm to peel off in sheets. When he awoke, his hand was bandaged afresh with linens, convalescing for further torture.

The town kept him just healthy enough, just lucid enough, to continue the torment.

He was persistently thirsty, always hungry, and there was always food and drink endlessly aplenty, set out on ornate banquet tables across the way. He first noticed it on his first day. Large hams strewn on silver platters, with sides of black-eyed peas and succotash and grilled chicken. Pitchers of frothing ale with dusty glasses of scotch to cleanse the palate.

But when he devoured and imbibed, nothing happened, his thirst was infinitely unquenchable, his appetite just as insatiable. The food and drink would usually morph in his mouth, sometimes transmuting to sand, sometimes to putrescent varmint, or cow manure. He ate nonetheless. This was the maddening happenstance of his days.

Besides the food and drink, there was one greater excruciation to Schinke, and that was his abject loneliness. Schinke desired to commune and to be in company with the human race he had so shunned, so recklessly injured.

He yearned for some conversation, human interaction, something, someone to keep him from going insane. Countless years passed in agony, until, one day, Steve the stallion remained outside. He didn't vanish, and was fastened to the wooden handrail where he had been seen so many times before.

Schinke rejoiced, shouted with glee, and approached his hoofed messiah. Joy transmogrified before his very eyes, turning into something hideously revolting, something which brought unbearable sorrow.

The animal was set upon by scores of demons, piling out of the houses like carnivorous locusts, tearing the creature limb from limb. They ate with bone crunching voraciousness, rending the meat between their serrated fangs, laughing all the while, spilling blood and viscera into the dampening earth.

Schinke fell to the ground, a broken-fragmented man. He kept repeating the words, "why, why, why," but no one answered him. The steam organ rang out, taunting his existence with every note materialized in the ether. He writhed in the dirt for a while, plotting an escape that would never come, his cheeks salted and mud caked in despair. The demoniacal horde retreated, slinking off into the metaphorical night that was always perpetual and whose darkness knew no end.

Darkness, in a place whose sun never set.

They left little of Steve. He was reduced to a splattering of bones and gristly flesh that littered the earth, an equine monument of desolation. Schinke crawled, on all fours, to the remains of his horse. The village was malicious, and had successfully transformed a once hardy outlaw into a groveling wretch. He lamented his steed, and while he mourned, he had an epiphany. There was no way out. The days continued.

An eternity of time passed. At least it seemed that long to the outlaw Schinke. The large looming clocktower revolved, its every tick and tock resounding through the town. It was unnoticeable at first, only the demon's calliope was, but soon it boomed, sonorously punc-tuating the hellish tune.

It was similar to the Chinese water torture he'd heard of during his years spent as a looter. The noise made his body convulse and throb in unbearable pain. His eyes felt as though they were bulging from the sockets. *Tick tock, tick, tock*, it continued, threatening to cave in his very skull.

One day, things changed and he began to see people. His prayers were seemingly answered: human interaction was nigh! From a distance he saw a little blonde girl, half her skull was missing, creating a yawning-misshapen countenance. It was from the head-shot wound he had administered years prior, when she was his hostage.

He glanced at a kind, mustachioed bank teller, whom he had stabbed to death for fun. And not for money. And he saw throngs of Comanche, Apache, and Kiowa that he had massacred with a blunt instrument in their sleep, and then scalped.

He saw more and more of his manifold victims. He cried out for their mercy... he just wanted some conversation; he just needed their voices. But they didn't speak, they only stared, then vanished in the curling wind. He whimpered, ensconced in the sweltering, unre-lenting humidity of the place.

The dampness of his tears being absorbed into the fourth dimension.

The spectral visitors came and went. Close, yet always far away, always out of reach, and never speaking.

He never knew how long he spent imprisoned, listening to the devil's calliope and the haunting clock clacking. The liquor he drank did absolutely nothing. The food he ate writhed with creeping maggots. His stomach turned, but he masticated it all the same. An insidious suffering coursed through his nervous system, dementing his stature. Schinke's hands were now consortiums of bones and charred flesh, remnants of the many times he went for his pistol.

He'd tried to converse with the calliope player, but the more he spoke to him the more terror pierced his adrenal glands and he would find himself trembling and crying out and pleading with him to stop tormenting him.

The demon's dermis was so red, redder than any chieftain's warpaint, and more deeply crimson than the center of the world. It panged Schinke to gaze upon. He could feel the coarseness of it, the wetness of it, grinding beneath the eyelids.

The days were the same with the sun burning eternal, a floating malevolence, cooking the town's bedeviled outlaw. Schinke had undergone the most hideous of transformations. Most of his teeth had rotted, and he made himself a hair doll named Frances that spoke to him and belittled him so he tore it apart.

One morning, Schinke heard the shambling patter of a wanderer's footsteps in the humid thoroughfare below. He crawled towards his window, freakishly emaciated and ghoulish in appearance. He surveyed the sun-soaked alley.

And he noticed a man who looked very lost, walking, limping, escorting a beat-up contraption that resembled a metal horse. The machine had two wheels comprised of crooked spokes and rubber with no tread. Its body was dented and dinged, blanketed in dust.

The strange beast lurched, its chipped contours made amorphous by the wear and tear of an unforgiving earth. It'd been traversing rough terrain, traveling the vast expanse to nowhere.

The man who brought it was disheveled and feral-looking, with a sun-beaten face and a big brown beard. His hair was long, mangled, protruding from his head like a patch of brambles. He wore a leather vest, stitched with the insignia of a winged skull. Schinke couldn't decipher the words around the symbol as he squinted. So, he decided to address the visitor.

"Who are you?" the outlaw Schinke shrieked from his bedroom vantage.

The man looked up. He saw a pair of seemingly disembodied, blood-red eyes. They glared down at him from a pitch-black, cavernous window.

"My name is Clovis. I just need a place to rest for a while."

The demon played his calliope, excited to claim another soul.

THE TALE OF REGINALD CLEAVER

Reginald Cleaver, age seven, pattered hither and thither through the plants of the greenhouse, weaving between Majesty Palms and Boston Ferns, his sneakers scuffed beyond any sort of recognition, his shoelaces untied and flapping like the ears of a shaggy dog.

He was giggling psychotically, holding a toy figurine who was partly melted and had half a face. His denim suspenders were caked with dirt and chocolate and unidentified condiments that'd missed his slobbering mouth.

Little Reginald scampered up to a potted palm and yoked one of its fronds from the trunk. He said, "*pluck!*" then scuttled to a bed of roses and began, systematically, to tear the petals from the flowers. Here was a red corolla, flung skyward, and there was a white one, and a yellow one. His pupils dilated and became deranged and although he was missing teeth, he gritted the ones that he had.

Feeling unsatiated in his blood, or sap-lust, Reginald skipped to his next victim. It was a Yuletide Camellia, with petals that were lushly pink, sporting a golden center of lavish fertility.

"*YOINK!*" he screamed as he tore all the pink from the flower, wresting away its brightness, leaving the thing a sad-green stalk. Now, it had only its golden pistil to show. Reginald then pinched the remaining yellow center of the flower and said: "*Oh, Gotcha!*"

He frolicked away... rushing up to the geraniums and orchids. He began massacring them as well. He even uprooted some bamboo stalks and snapped them in two over his knee. As Reginald reached for a Singapore Orchid's last luscious petal, which was a regal-purplish beaut, flecked with white, an old man, the horticulturist of said greenhouse, snatched up his hand and constricted it in his own, his eyes filling with anger.

"WHADDYA THINK YOU'RE DOING!" he chastised the child. "WHY WOULD YOU HURT THESE HARMLESS CREATURES!? How would you like it if someone came up to you, and PULLED ALL YOUR FINGERS OFF!!!"

The boy wailed without rhythm, as though he'd swallowed a jumble of instruments. He was trying to alert *someone*.

And that someone came.

A big, haughty woman strode between the tortured foliage, stepping with strained high heels upon discarded fronds, shredded leaves, and snapped twigs. She was wearing a large sundress, embroidered with cartoony tulips.

"What is the meaning of all this!?" she squealed. "Unhand my child at once!"

She struck the elderly horticulturist, hitting him over the head with her large handbag. It connected with a *thunk* and, wincing in pain, the man let go.

The woman huffed, sticking out her chest in a snooty, entitled sort of way.

"I have half a mind to call the police! You'd be locked away like that." She snapped her fingers. "For harming my sweet boy!"

The horticulturist was stunned into silence.

"Come on, Reginald," the woman said, taking her son's hand. "Let's go get you some ice cream."

As she shepherded her child away, hurrying, storming with rage, Reginald looked over his shoulder and stuck his tongue out, taunting the trembling old man.

Soon, their blue minivan peeled out of the parking lot at a high velocity, cutting directly into traffic.

"That uppity negro should learn to mind his own business," Reginald's mother snarled.

Suddenly, a battering ram of a big rig, carrying tons of lumber, careened into them from the side, causing a blossoming, fiery explosion that killed Reginald and his mother instantly.

The old man began sweeping pieces of torn shrubbery and refuse into his tiny dustpan.

His good ear still ringing from the handbag, he didn't hear the crash.

REGINALD AWOKE with his legs firmly rooted in the moist soil of a big plastic pot. He was stuck there, unable to move, yet still able to feel the pain coursing through his body. A dank, anguished breeze wafted through the place, reeking of spoiled meat and botflies. It stung his nose.

Flanking him on both sides were more and more children, as well as a few adults. They were all seemingly, similarly, in the same captured state.

His hands were outstretched, his fingers splayed, tightly wrapped with string to secure them to a matrix of sticks. His back ached, as straight as a ruler, because of a stake driven in the dirt behind him. He was fastened to it, as well.

He could move his mouth, sort of, but could not turn his head. Hearing whispers manifold, he wrangled a while with his lips and mustered out a meek, "Hullo..."

Eventually, he heard the creaking of tropical vines, then the rustling of brambles in a glen, then a hushed *schwooping* noise, like a shambling tumbleweed composed of arid thorns.

And eventually, he saw an unpotted palm, walking upon its spidery roots, shuffling, dragging its dirty tentacles on the ground. It was approaching him.

The plant was about his height, or would be, if the boy wasn't elevated and wedged in a pot. It studied Reginald, who in turn breathed rapidly, shutting his eyes so no light could break through.

The plant slowly outstretched a few of its fronds, lithely wrapping them around Reginald's finger, and: "*YANK!*"

Reginald screamed, his eyes now big, brimming with fright. The plant outstretched some more of its fronds, enwrapping his pinky finger, then his thumb, and the wind said: "*YOINK!*" and "*Oh, Gotcha!*"

Reginald caterwauled like a well-bound banshee. He was being ogled by the other prisoners; all of which were relieved they weren't being mangled at the moment.

Swallowing, feeling immense pain, the boy spotted more leafy torturers waiting in line.

An orchid, a beautiful creamy azure, with majestic petals; a natural bouquet of technicolored carnations; some daffodils; begonias; geraniums; a prickly hydrangea bush; a radish; even a few stalks of bamboo.

They took turns, violently wrenching appendages from the sadist's grubby hands.

Slowly, the nubbins wriggled, then grew back to fingers. An auspicious event, since the line was unquestionably long, and many were the flora who wanted to claim extremities. Reginald shrieked for the first ten centuries. Then he became like the others, comatose and dull.

MEANWHILE, Miss Cleaver yelped in a room adjoining hell's greenhouse. The line wrapped twelve times around the known multiverse, which was never-ending. Scores of mistreated peoples waited patiently, to slap her with a very large handbag.

TIN BULLET
FROM OUTER SPACE!

Whitaker, Hernandez, Bailey, Hayes, Ogawa, Oblonsky. Four Americans. One Japanese. One Russian. The best the current world had to offer.

One half-scientist, one half-daredevil, bent toward suicide.

And so, they went...

The astronauts erupted from the ground in their TIN BULLET, thrusting up and through the atmosphere while a propulsive jet of ruddy, orange flame shot down and homeward toward earth. They would never be landbound again. Their cheeks pulled back and their eyelids disappeared into their sockets, making their expressions insane.

They clung to the armrests of their seats while the silver space-suits hugged their bodies like insulating pillows. And they broke through the outermost layers of atmosphere—as an arriving baby breaks through the membranes—and pulled their thrusters down 'till the orange flame licked out against black space and vanished.

"Ready boys!" said the gray-haired Captain Whitaker.

"We were born ready, Captain! Let's see what this *Tin Bullet* can fucking DO!" said Hernandez. He was sweating so much, his space-man's cap had glommed onto his shaven scalp.

THE GIANT HAD LAID another egg. It was the size of LAX's parking garage, cream-colored with green and purple polka dots. It landed from beneath the thing's legs. It was the seventh egg laid so far across the Americas, and this one, like the eggs before it, killed many.

The giant stood five-hundred feet tall. As it walked, it crushed neighborhoods and flattened area codes. Guns were of no use, no matter the size, the rounds would bounce off of the giant's very blue shins.

In fact, its whole body was very blue. And it was hermaphroditic, since it had male sex organs and plopped eggs out of a cloaca-like orifice in its perineum-vulva.

Atop its massive shoulders sat a bulge lined with many rows of teeth. And when the *creature* opened its mouth, a humongous eyeball could be seen staring from the back of its tongue.

Circling planes rattled their artillery and blasted their rockets, noticing the monster, which purportedly emerged from behind a tectonic plate in the Yucatan, had arms and wings and tentacles extending from its sides.

When the wings fluttered, forests were blown away. When the tentacles flailed, buildings exploded. When the arms swiped, a similar result followed, and a lot of people died.

The monster seemed to be making its way up from Mexico to Texas, across the United States to the east coast, making pit stops to lay eggs and eat trees and inhale lakes.

IN A STATE OF NERVOUSNESS, the astronauts glanced at one another and smiled. But it was an empty gesture, unable to hide the angst-hued sadness in their eyes, nor the palpable fear suffusing the ship's cabin as they rocketed towards something dangerous, and hungry.

Yet they had to do it. This was the only chance that their children, wives, husbands, and friends, would go on. It was the only chance for *Earth*.

At least, that's what they believed.

Bailey began reorienting the craft, pushing her hands to levers that turned the tin contraption until it was traveling parallel with the planet. Going at orbital velocity, along with satellites, cosmological pebbles, and space stations, they rocketed at 7,000 miles per hour. And this was without their thrusters.

"We're almost in position, Captain," she said.

"Very well... What do you make of it, Ogawa? We're hedging all of our bets on this plan," said Whitaker.

"It will work," replied Ogawa. "It has to."

Ogawa had invented and amalgamated the metal to engineer the craft—exporting minerals from mines miles down in South Africa and had then tempered the component parts with tungsten, titanium, lead, cobalt, uranium.

And, of course, tin.

That's how the ship got its name. For it looked like a muddled gray bullet, flying through the black void. Oblonsky eyed the radar, sweat poured from his brow and down his long nose.

"NOW!" he yelled.

Hernandez and Hayes depressed a series of buttons on their instrument panels. The engine roared alive and blue flame streamed from the back of the ship. Twenty-thousand miles per hour. And then thirty. Forty. They gripped their seats, and they prayed and remembered their families.

IT WAS CURRENTLY in the mountain town of Pigeon Forge, Tennessee. Home of Dolly Parton.

They'd thought about nuking it, but concluded that it might worsen their odds, since it seemed to absorb much of the fire thus far. Gaining steam. Every shot seemed to morph the skeletal structure of its hideous body. Making it even bluer. And ornerier.

Also, nuking it would probably kill a lot of people.

Its skin seemed impenetrably cut from primeval diamond; the world noticed that once the equally adamantine eggs hatched, chances for survival were limited.

This is where Ogawa and the five other astronauts came in. The spacecraft's material, according to the Japanese metallurgist/engineer, could pierce the animal's hide.

He assured those with a bended ear that the space bullet could, and would, kill the monster. It just had to come from outer space—it just had to pierce its heart. It also had to travel at unfathomable speeds.

They made their calculations, and built the spaceship in a hurry.

The crew blasted off and circled the earth at an ever-intensifying velocity. The beast down below tore through the Dollywood theme park—swallowing those in the Mystery Mine, stamping out the entirety of the FireChaser Express, and swatting down the Wild Eagle —after grabbing its steel tracks and twisting them 'round like a pipe cleaner, devouring some still on the ride.

The monster gorged itself on the suffering of Earth's inhabitants.

It flapped its hulking wings and made tinder of the remaining concession stands and gift shops and orange restrooms. It soared, flanked on both sides by F-22 Raptors, with frightened pilots who prayed that the thing would land in the woods, somewhere far away from the rest of civilization.

THE TIN BULLET was rocketing at 70,000 miles per hour. The hull was white-hot and holding, and although all aboard were nervously glued to their seats, its durability provided some comfort.

"We can't dive down yet. It's moving too fast... to what looks like Vermont," said Bailey.

"Vermont? Just what the heck is this thing?" replied Captain Whitaker.

"It does not think like you or I," said Ogawa. "We would obviously go to the White House, or to Times Square, to reap the most damage. But the creature, well, it seems to be confused."

"What you getting at!?" barked Oblonsky in his Russian drawl.

"It hasn't seen the Earth for a few billion years," Ogawa replied. "It does not know what we are or where it is. Hypotheses abound of it hibernating in a stasis beneath the planet's crust. And now, maybe it's as frightened as we are. Maybe it's just reacting to our guns."

"Says inventor of Tin fucking Bullet designed to explode its heart!?" squalled Oblonsky

"Just an idea," said Ogawa.

"Well, keep ideas to yourself!"

"Everyone, cool it, now! The world down there is depending on us, and if we screw this up, well, there won't be anyone to depend on anything anymore," remarked Captain Whitaker.

The radar screen before Bailey operated much like those in submarines and it began *pinging* with an echoing tinny sound.

"Sir! It seems to have landed in Coney Island! It's dragging its feet through the boardwalk as we speak!" said Bailey.

"Good Lord! How long 'till we have a clear trajectory, Bailey!?" asked Captain Whitaker, gritting his perfectly symmetrical teeth.

"I estimate approximately three-and one-half minutes, sir! At this speed, we're revolving around the earth once every five and a half minutes. We're almost in position!"

Whitaker slowly appraised the astronauts within the TIN BULLET, pausing thoughtfully on each and every variform face.

Hernandez was praying the *Ave Maria!* clutching the beads of his olivewood rosary, rolling them through his perspiring thumb and forefinger. Hayes, a veteran of three foreign wars, kept repeating the words *Hoorah! Hoorah! Hoorah!* under his breath. His neck muscles flexed in a rippling of fibrous blood-tissues as his adrenaline spiked.

Whitaker prepared himself. He'd been mentally rehearsing his speech for a few months, but he'd sprinkle in a few improvisations. That's how good he was.

"Despite the most recent argument, which is understandable, I can honestly say that you all are the most daring men and women I have ever met. I know we will die in a few moments, as is the plan, but the needs of the many outweigh the needs of the few. So, I just want to say, on behalf of the United States and all the denizens of Planet Earth, thank you for your sacrifice," monologued Whitaker.

No one was paying close attention. Bailey nodded a few times, focusing on the control panel and the radar—staring intently and stoically as her eyes narrowed behind her glasses and she slowly maneuvered the controls of the bullet.

Ogawa, on the other hand, remained pensive and wondered if his creation was the right approach. He remembered the kamikazes his country had produced nearly a century before, and he balked at the ironic idea of being the same—in an era where that level of unthinking and sacrificial suicide was frowned upon in the mainland.

He'd designed a bullet when bullets had been proven not to work. And yes, it might be capable of piercing the monster's dermis, but who's to know where its heart, or hearts, actually are? They'd all just guessed its location.

Maybe he'd struck a truthful chord when he said the monster was simply confused. Maybe it wasn't lashing out in malice, but in a sort of defensive reflex to a plethora of new stimuli.

It didn't matter now. It was too late to turn back, and too late to unbuild the Tin Bullet scrap by ill-intentioned scrap. Captain Whitaker began his rendition of the Star-Spangled Banner:

Ooooh, say does that star-spangled banner yet waaaaave!! Foor the Laand of the Freeeeee and the Hooooome of the Braave!!"

He was, indeed, a vestige of a bygone era. A tear wetted his cheek as the Tin Bullet dipped downward and began hurtling at unimaginable speeds through the atmospheric layers. Whitaker instructed all to put on their helmets and gloves, "Just in case!" he said.

His wrinkled hands patted the pristine part of his gray head. His eyes were somber, earnest, and scared. He lamented the inevitability of never seeing his wife, nor his children, nor his grandchildren again.

Whitaker withdrew a silver locket from his empty spaceman's glove.

He'd squirreled it away in secret, just like he always had during his decades among the stars in the near-endless chasm of the universe. With a rutted thumb, he clicked the locket open, beholding an image of his wife and he, fifty years before, smiling without a care in the world, standing on a balmy beach in Honolulu. It was their honeymoon. He wished he could go there now.

"*HOORAH!!*" declared Hayes, next to Whitaker. He shut his eyes, and tried to breathe.

Everyone clicked their bubble-helmets into place. They slid thick gloves onto their hands and snapped them into the suit as well. They tore through the stratosphere and the mesosphere, and Ogawa couldn't shake the feeling that this was all wrong.

They passed through the clouds in a blurring hodgepodge of metallic fire and the interface in front of Bailey *chirped-chirped-chirped*, as it homed in on the spot where the monster's heart was believed to be.

The giant, moments before, wrested a Nathan's hotdog venue from the asphalt and began munching on it like it was a pig in a blanket. Its mouth swallowing all. Its eye understanding nothing.

A SMALL CHILD NAMED MAYA, who wore twin buns and a pink and white dress, had broken away from her mother amid the chaos of the giant's landing. Her mother sobbed frantically while herds of beachgoers and pedestrians blew past, too desperate to hear her pleas.

NYPD officer, Nikolas Balaban, wrestled his way through the crowd, as rubble rained down on the shoreline and the monster took its time destroying everything in sight.

Balaban's PTSD flared up as he remembered the terrorist attacks of decades before.

He'd witnessed the same pandemonium—the same collective scrambling of a citizenry tormented by so much fear and confusion. Everyone fought to survive. And everyone fought to save each other.

Balaban saw a little girl walking dazed among the throng. And he heard a woman screaming close by for someone to: "SAVE MY CHILD! MAYA! SOMEONE, PLEASE, SAVE HER!"

Soon, the girl stood at the hideous and blue clubbed foot of the monster that'd impressed itself on the beach. Balaban ran to her, overriding his PTSD, as the snarling freak glanced down, and its thousands of teeth glistened ravenous.

With a swipe of its tentacle, Balaban was gone. And a red vapor lingered in his place. He would be remembered as a hero.

A ROAR RESOUNDED. An orange flame zipped through the afternoon sky so quickly that the crew of the Tin Bullet had no time to react before the vessel crashed below the sternum of the giant.

It punched its way through the animal's deep flesh, slowing considerably as it did so, until it was traveling at 75, 65, 55 miles per hour. It cut into an arrhythmic and atypical purple heart. The crew found themselves sequestered in a purplish-roiling liquid within one of its ventricles.

Every thudding palpitation of the huge heart crushed the Tin Bullet more and more and the crew braced themselves in a stupor, listening to the monster bellowing from the other side. The little girl moved closer.

"It worked!" yelled Oblonsky.

Ogawa said nothing. He peered to his left to see Captain Whitaker unconscious with a broken neck. Hernandez had died. His harness snapped on impact and he lay mangled halfway in and halfway out of his sparking control panel. Bailey shook and muttered insensibly to herself about some calculations. A piece of metal had cut through her shoulder.

The heart compressed and compressed; the Bullet crunched beneath its weight like a soda can.

"Oblonsky!" screamed Ogawa. "I think it's hurt! Can you make it to Captain Whitaker's station? My legs... they're broken!"

"It worked?" yelled Oblonsky.

"I don't know, listen..." Ogawa spit up blood. The Tin Bullet was buckling from the pressure and began acid pouring through its breaches, sizzling upon the interior of the craft.

"Go to Whitaker's station and punch in the code. We need to detonate! Now!"

"So, you're saying it worked!?" Oblonsky jittered and stared at Ogawa. His eyes had gone mad.

"Listen to me, damnit! Go!"

The vessel creaked and moaned as a steady stream of the burning substance leaked in. It fell directly on Oblonsky, who was still asking if the plan had worked. He shrieked, then, with the acid eating through both his suit and marrow, he died.

Hayes, who slumped unconscious next to Hernandez, fell apart next, his limbs coming off in strings of sizzling mush and disintegrating muscle.

Ogawa jostled with his harness. Bailey continued muttering and then cogently unclipped herself. She stepped over the pooling acid as the walls came in and she pointed to a series of buttons before the dead Captain.

"These!?" she asked.

"YES!!" screamed Ogawa. She nodded and punched in the code.

OUTSIDE, amid the terror and bedlam, the monster spasmed and clutched its chest. Then, it belched with indigestion. A little cloud of smoke exited from between its teeth. The giant roared so loud that the clouds dispersed overhead. Maya looked up at the great beast, feeling compassion imbue her childlike essence. The thing looked down at her and prepped a tentacle.

Suddenly, she hugged its toe. Nothing but a mere ant on a leviathan log. She hugged and hugged and cried. "It's ok, monster," she said. "I love you, everything will be ok, don't be scared."

The giant heaved and it opened and closed its mouth. It extended a long green tongue through its pointed teeth. They both stood there. They felt one another, and the world grew silent.

"Don't worry, Mr. Monster. It's all ok, I promise. Nothing to be afraid of here. Nothing at all."

The girl kept squeezing the toe, the speck that she was, and she smiled and rubbed her cheek on it. The giant made a strange huffing noise, like that of a wounded horse overblown in size. It stepped back and away from the girl, toward the ocean and the setting sun.

"I love you, Mr. Monster!" she called after it and it looked back at her, opening its humongous mouth so the eye could fully see. It now understood. And its fear dissipated.

Dorsal fins beetled on the creature's back before it dove into the water. The girl waved, and said, "Bye, Mr. Monster. We love you!"

The giant lifted from the water but once, then fell, never to surface again.

And the eggs didn't hatch. For now.

STEEL DRAGON

There were three trains operating in tandem on the snaking steel tracks, wrapping twistingly around an empty expanse of sky. There were four cars conjoined within each train and within the train-cars, sixteen thrill-seekers sat upright in tense twosomes, nervous, ready.

They were abreast from one another, and as said, giddy or scared, but rarely, very seldomly, were they coolly or wholly indifferent.

Here, they were clacked down upon by the alligator mouth of a double-sided harness. The yoke was pushed and clicked into place, circumventing the riders' grinning, soon-to-be-concussed heads.

Fatigued staff members shuffled by and by, checking the seatbelts and other safety machinations.

They gently prodded at the apparatuses, mirage-like materials spinning the illusory web of normalcy. A weariness beyond the carnies' years riddled their drooping, sagging faces, as the toll of another, and another, and another day at Thrills-Ville Amusement Park dawned upon them. Their indifference was in sharp contrast with the serpentine ride, with its enormousness, its sheer death-defying whips, pivots, loops, and drops. One hundred and twenty-eight miles per hour. Zero to that speed in a flickering three and a half seconds, spanning trestles that stretched precariously on for one point nine miles. It was an adrenaline junkie's mecca. The brave few, now strapped to their seats, were in for an interesting experience.

The long train consisted of steel and aluminum alloys, built for sleekness, for speed. The lead car, a battering ram against wind and elements, was molded, blowtorched, and crafted to resemble a snarling, soaring, bewhiskered Chinese reptile of ancient lore—its eyes meting out equal parts peril and destruction.

This face would ferry the passengers irrevocably to their fates, onwards and upwards towards destinies not necessarily confined to the metal intestines on which they were now shackled, soon to spin and dart through heights unimaginable, dangerous. They smiled.

This was, The Steel Dragon.

At Thrills-Ville, all rollercoasters, all mechanical amusements, are put on a thirty-minute hiatus after the crackling whip of a thunderclap. This spans indefinitely, if the storm continues roiling, burgeoning, churning cylindrical tempests in the heavens. Lightning is bad for business.

And yet, this specific squall was just now budding and percolating, doubling over from within itself onto itself, with fat clouds—blue, grey, black, and purple—levitating amongst the backdrop of an unfeeling horizon. It was a conjurer's storm belonging to a voodoo priestess, and it swept in like an apocalyptic avalanche, suffocating those unlucky few in its wake.

The rollercoaster took off, zipping up a steep ascent into the mouth of the inclement weather. The passengers were enshrouded in a blanket of clouds; the ride paused momentarily, then dropped abruptly, blurring human and machine, lurching with a sudden clangor that rocked bodies and put stomachs in throats and pinioned heads to backboards. The force of gravity was quick. Powerful. The coaster spiraled through space, football fields in length, and it rocketed back upwards, once again cresting the tumultuous skies.

A sharp left turn, and then a right, followed by three consecutive backflips of growing circular orbits. Then a speedy straightaway, halfway done now, the Steel Dragon preempted for its grand finale.

Lightning.

It made a zigging descent through the blue-black sky, alighting on the rollercoaster, hellishly constricting the train cars and passengers. Myriad sparks were seen, yellow currents wrapping around the steely conduit, creating sibilant hissing, searing whispers that resounded as if through a megaphone.

The rollercoaster slowed slightly while being electrocuted, and the sixteen passengers, all manacled to their alloyed coffins, rocked back and forth, spasming wildly, their complexions melding with the steel surrounding them.

It was a brilliant transformative display; they were now burnt and charred, fleshy-tangerine pinks and violets, writhing and flailing bodies, limbs, appendages conjoined, irrevocably, with the metal beast.

The rollercoaster free-fell down a precipitous descent, then scaled up and over a hillock of trestles. The passengers, now mutated globs of silvering flesh, shrieked and keened with indecipherable shrillness.

At a sudden bend, the Steel Dragon refused to veer left. Keeping up its forward momentum, it careered off the predetermined tracks, sundering itself forever. Those still in line witnessed the soon-to-be collision, waited for the inevitable impact of metal on cement.

At the last moment, the rollercoaster pulled up.

It *soared*.

It slithered inexplicably through the air. It ascended, rippling with lithe undulations, a monster that should not exist, a reptilian cretin of ancient lore. A Dragon. And it swooped, absconding from vision, the passengers now mere ridges on the back, wailing mounds of teeth within liquescent coagulating skin, inhuman stegosaurus-like plates, warty steeple-countenances aligning the train cars.

They were scalps and twisted mouths and viscous eyeballs. They were a macabre picket fence. They were made to be the spine of the new species. And yet, they were not the spine. They had become a gestalt, a new mind all together, freakishly misshapen mutants, dead-yet-alive parts of a whole. Organs of the monster. They had become the consciousness. They were now the brain.

They were not themselves.

There were no more personalities. The thing was devoid of individuals. Shedding their humanly sheaths for something far more hideous, immensely more grotesque, their wails sliced through the midsummer air. A singular suffering had been singed into their synapses, contemporaneously, while their flesh was being sutured to the ride.

All in the amusement park screamed while the squall smothered all lingering sunshine, drawing a curtain over the land, to let everyone know the bubble had popped; the theater depicting relative safety had ended.

Thrills-Ville was now on involuntary pause: the electrical switches, lever, cams, and sprockets all lay impotently still.

The short-circuiting suspended people aloft in midair, or upside-down and locked in, dangling wildly, ensnared in devices that no longer protected them. They were undergoing a transformation much different than the unlucky sixteen.

Unable to run or defend themselves, the trapped individuals had become pieces of bait. If the skies were the seas, then they would be replete with fresh chum, waiting expectantly for a soaring shark, a predatorial beast, a monster.

The Steel Dragon circled back, swimming through the purpling sky, somehow still flying: a new, improved, apex predator.

It set its sights on the lazy river within the waterpark subsection of the larger Thrills-Ville. The people were unaware of the hazard orbiting overhead, and the lifeguards were nowhere to be seen, having abandoned all posts in a sudden flurry. The dragon made a looping semicircle like a vulture, then tipped its snout down, traveling headlong for the river.

Gasps came first.

Then came the screams.

The swimmers commenced scrambling, climbing over each other's shoulders, desperately trying to survive. It was too late. Electricity shot from the Steel Dragon's mouth in ebbing, flowing waves, suffusing the water to cook everything, and everyone, it held.

Shocked to death, the corpses floated supine and prone, congregating like boiled jetsam, brimming the edges of the lazy river with a bunch of popped, yellow inner tubes.

The dragon billowed away from the site, focusing on a drop tower called The Kerplunk. The amusement, once blinking fluorescently, was now dead and darkened, rising like a tall gravestone one hundred and fifteen-feet in height.

At capacity, it held thirty-passengers up to the bloodthirsty sky.

The sedentary sacrifices, held in place by the tower's air compression system, were stuck, and could do nothing but wince.

And scream.

They wished for the sharp drop, wished for escape, their adrenal glands pumping, a ubiquitous flight response activated; yet locked in, strapped down, unable to flee. They were so high up, so trapped, so defenseless in their circular gondola. The Steel Dragon snaked its way among the clouds, a menacing slither from so large an anomaly. It bore in.

The pinned-down group let out a collective howl, then an asynchronous, arrhythmic one as they shook their harnesses, desperately jerking with failing might. Those that could see stared wide-eyed at the unfortunate happenings. They saw the glinting steel beast whipping towards them. It was strangely sadistic.

One person escaped: a petite Slinky of a woman, she managed to wriggle free. One hundred and two feet. She fell until that final moment, where she met her splattering crescendo.

The rest, lovebirds, thrill-seekers, siblings, cousins, neighbors, friends, held hands. Some shut their eyes. Others did not. There the monstrosity was, with its immobile mouth open. This was it.

The Steel Dragon collided head-on with The Kerplunk, shattering the tower into a million irreparable pieces. It exploded with scarlet definitiveness. The crash echoed, shifting molecules in the air, puncturing the innermost ear canals of sprinting bystanders, while delivering twisted hunks of shrapnel to the frightened multitude below.

The monster had bestowed the riders with their drop, even though it was different from the one they'd imagined.

Lionized by the incident, the Dragon flew further, keen on spreading its agenda of destruction. It incinerated those cowering beneath the funnel cake stand, the ring toss, and the adjoining balloon-and-dart.

The monster barreled through the revolving Viking longship, cutting it in two like a kraken, then toppled the Ferris wheel, spraying its inhabitants asunder. It dismantled the Tilt-a-Whirl in three swooping arcs. It electro-bombed a partially evacuated carousel, sending wood horses zipping aflame in every direction, their riders now dead.

The Dragon leveled the Rotor, previously named the Rotating Rumble-Strip; it tore through the Haunted Mansion, demolishing the edifice; it broke down the Scrambler and made the Log-O-Riffic Rides run red; it upended the bumper cars; it went into the parking lot and careened into vehicles; it murdered more with electricity; and then it flew away, over the steeples of tall evergreens.

THE STEEL DRAGON slinked its way into Philadelphia. The monster, unperturbed by gunfire, dodging missiles, destroyed the United States Mint. The military upped their offense, compounding their weaponization with semi-automatics, sniper rifles, and M1A2 SEP tanks.

The tanks rolled indolently into striking distance, as if their treaded wheels were submerged in treacle. They pivoted the cannons perched on the rooftops, but didn't fire them; it was too risky, there was too much infrastructure. The soldiers continued unloading their guns, round after round, with little luck.

The bullets simply ricocheted, pinging from the underbelly of the rollercoaster's train cars—the munitions slicing through limbs, store windows, cars, and thoroughfares. And the Dragon moved fast, flittering here one moment, then suddenly, it was three to four blocks away, often traveling through the facades of buildings, rather than going around them.

It left Philadelphia in ruins, and through oral electrical currents, it left many of its denizens smeared, with skin resembling bubbling Cheese Whiz amidst fragmented portions of tumbled-down architecture.

It traveled to Jersey.

It click-clacked amongst the skyline, reveling in its position as a self-proclaimed wrecking ball, a circuitous purveyor of a baleful doom. The unwieldy cretin brought innumerable buildings to their metaphorical knees, nothing left save rubble and crag. Entire blocks flattened into unrecognizable refuse, streaking the industrial ambience with ungainly gliding maneuvers, it went on to the next stop, on its East Coast tour.

It was in New York City, in Times Square, that The Steel Dragon met its would-be-slayer. Opposites are a reality; this is true in physics as well as in the ethereal world. Every yin has its yang, and as such, on the reverse side of an anemic invalid is a Mister or Misses Universe.

Therefore, every scourge needs its elixir; every pestilence needs a serum to combat that bane of humanity, which in this case, was a rollercoaster enlivened through electrical galvanism, now possessing the ability to shoot electricity from its mouth, writhing with wart-like heads for reptilian spinal ridges.

The opposite of such an unspeakable deformity, a peculiar aeronautical alien of the highest order, could only be terrain-bound, frail, and wholly unimpressive. It should be laughable, and supremely goofy in the face of something so fear-inducing.

With a scrawny, weak build, as opposed to the metallic, seemingly impenetrable train cars. And a pointed, pinched-up face, contrasting the Steel Dragon's ominous expression.

And that's what Don Miguel Rigoberto de Ruiz was.

An enfeebled octogenarian who lived in a nursing home in Staten Island. He was purported to have dementia and, in his more hoary-headed years, claimed himself to be the physical embodiment of Cervantes's Don Quixote, the purveyor of chivalry, the battler of windmills.

Don Miguel's only similarity to Don Quixote was that they both originated from Spain. One wasn't real. Two weren't real according to the nursing home staff, who felt Miguel was an enchanting and passionate man who lived in a world of his own imagining.

The aged old scarecrow studied the Steel Dragon on the television screen, in the common area, encircled by elders fiddling with baccarat or mahjong or checkers, flipping through sheaves of postcards or snoring into expired newspapers.

The television was a small and blocky 28-inches; it unveiled a blurred montage of granulated images bespeaking bedlam. But the multicolored pictures, somehow, delved deep into the pit of the senior citizen's soul.

Everything moved into place slowly, yet inexorably, fitting comfortably within the mind of the old Spaniard. His brain, previously scattered, was now a completed picture, an enlightened jigsaw puzzle of reveries and once-idling thoughts. Don Miguel decided, there, in the common area of Codger Life Estates, that The Steel Dragon was just the adventure he needed to show the world his mettle.

He escaped that night, elucidated by the moon, and he went to a nearby farm belonging to a well-to-do horticulturist. He shimmied himself between two loose two-by-fours that were splintering and warped and were barely enclosing the barn.

Getting in wasn't difficult, given the skinniness of his frame and the tiredness of the partitions. He tiptoed around, blind as a mouse, groping in the dark until he found what he was looking for: the farm owner's horse. He pilfered it and most everything else, including the saddle and a bag of grass, for equine sustenance.

After pushing the stable door open from within, he shepherded the animal to freedom. Soon, Don Miguel became flabbergasted.

What he believed to be a stallion in the dark, turned out to be a mare by dawn. It was mottled with black spots upon an otherwise ivory-white coat of fur. It was a pinto. It was quick, too, hellishly so.

The old man mounted the steed when at a safe distance from the barn and when obscured by wooded forests. He commenced traveling for three and a half hours, via horseback, towards the city.

He traversed the Verrazano-Narrows Bridge from Staten Island to Brooklyn. And then the Manhattan Bridge into Manhattan (rather than taking the Brooklyn Bridge, which didn't have a cycling path).

Now he was here, in Manhattan, alone, elevated from the ground on stolen hooves, his sharp face bending the foreboding winds, his skinny Fu-Manchu swaying with the air currents.

He had been in this place before, but never by medieval means of transportation, and never under the pressing thumb of such dreadful circumstances. Don Miguel noticed how much the city had changed since his thirty-and-some-year absence.

For one, it was being evacuated. He used the circumstances to his advantage, moving in opposing directions, against the grain from wherever pedestrians were running. In many ways, he had ended up in Manhattan with a zigzagging effect, by a calculating default, and not by a whim.

Don Miguel surveyed the vacuous storefronts. They looked like futuristic caves, most likely with grunting proprietors. He wondered about Neanderthals, then, pondering their motives in selling "I LOVE NY" T-shirts and paperweight trinkets depicting a miniaturized Statue of Liberty. It didn't make sense. Nothing did, not anymore. Many stores had signs that read, "CLOSED FOR BUSINESS" while others flaunted broken windows, an unfortunate side-effect of nihilistic looters, who were capitalizing on The Steel Dragon's presence.

The city looked like a necropolis now, and it was fitting since Don Miguel felt like a ghost having an out-of-body experience, treading away down trash-littered thoroughfares, astride his phantasmal mare, its spectral tail whooshing out glops of ectoplasm.

Maybe, Don Miguel was tired.

He drew his steed to a halt, then climbed arthritically down off his horse. The elder still wore his flowy, gown-like pajama-wear, spangled with knitworks of palm trees and pineapples. He felt he needed new attire, something that made him less of a target, less vulnerable, something that looked better, something that was more appropriate to wear when one does battle with a dragon.

The shop he entered was a weapons emporium and antique shop, mostly of outdated embattled artifacts, on display for the curious passerby and the serious collector alike.

Stepping over foot-long shards of glass, he inched his way around overturned displays, rubbing his bald pate, fingering his facial whiskers and the white, wispy hairs he still had on his temples and behind his ears.

He studied the ransacked and broken surroundings, ferreting, clambering, rummaging through the store, casing the uninhabitable place for something he might be able to use.

He found nothing at first, so he went deeper, setting his bleary sights on a storage room, seemingly for unsold wares and undesir-ables. It was within the dingy, light-flickered wardrobe, abutting a yellowing mop bucket and some electrical equipment, that he discov-ered a partial suit of armor.

There shone a helmet, replete with visor and comb, a segmented gorget for neck safety, pauldrons for the shoulders, metallic double-jointed gauntlets for the hands, and a chromium-gilded breastplate, with a seven-foot lance leaning against it.

"Hmmm," he said as he put the suit of armor on.

Don Miguel loped from the antiquity emporium, tiptoeing in his slip-on espadrilles, maneuvering himself between tumbled-down shelves and glass encasements with the panache of an eccentric conquistador.

He was a hodgepodge of a human being, an anachronism from an era long gone, yet still himself, in the common day; both a pastiche of a fictional knight, who himself was a fictional knight, and a dementia-addled senior citizen, unwilling or unable to coordinate his clothing.

He clicked and clacked with a rickety momentum, narrowing his eyes on his dalmatian-like pinto, who was waiting by the entrance-way. He sidestepped and ducked and then stepped some more, until he tripped upon a ram's-horn trumpet. It was a curved piece of keratin-bone, previously protruding from the head of a proud animal.

"I could use this," Don Miguel thought while he hoisted himself up, along with the trumpet, lance, and armor.

He scuttled like a tinman, escaping the shop, arduously humming through gritted and capped teeth, pushing his armored chest outward, even though it weighed a perceived ton.

He let his helm roll back between his shoulders while his myopic-black eyes surveyed the blue heavens, aiming his goateed chin to the skyline like a focusing telescope. He was sure, now, he was the dragon slayer. Don Miguel shuffled up to his horse, whom he decided was named Rocinante, and mounted the hoofed transport with much difficulty.

It was uneasy going, having to lug his heavy new belongings. Don Miguel felt like a turtle imprisoned within a shell of iron. His armor heated with the sun's rays, baking the old man within.

The armor felt both cumbersome and uncomfortable, yet Don Miguel was safe... Or at least he hoped. Sweating like a wrung-out sponge, he had an epiphany, a eureka moment. The rollercoaster must also be baking in the sun, rotting, decomposing. It was part flesh, after all, with all of the heads and disparate appendages of its absorbed victims.

So, he broke into a grocery store, ravening and gathering loaves of bread and some charcuterie: turkey, salami, mortadella, liverwurst. He also grabbed some water, which he would use to quench not only his thirst but that of Rocinante.

He remounted the pinto and trotted with purpose down 7th Avenue, just eight blocks away from the intersection with W 47th Street and Times Square.

On the way, he feasted, like a starving goblin on the filched charcuterie, leaving crumbs and flecks of deli meat within his goatee and on the asphalt surrounding him. He slurped at the water, permitting slavering rivulets to crest and spill from his chapped lips, then down his emaciated cheeks, flowing under his breastplate, creating a humidity unlike any he'd ever known—worse even, than the time the air conditioning broke in the middle of July at Codger Life Estates.

His friend, whom he'd called Sancho, had suffered a heat stroke.

Don Miguel dropped little pieces of bread beside Rocinante,

rubbing them to smithereens between the desiccated, soft tips of his fingers. Soon, he'd attracted a crowd.

Laughing gulls cawed and flew alongside him, starboard to the mare, run-of-the-mill seagulls followed suit, arching down then back up again in ellipses of rapturous fluttering. Don Miguel kicked the heels of his slippers into Rocinante's flanks, and the two went on.

Grinning with yellowing veneers, tarnished from too much espresso, he then heard The Steel Dragon.

It was barreling through story after story of architectural achievement, making skirling, screeching noises, pursuing its urge for destruction. Unfettered, Don Miguel trod on, feeding himself and his gulls, making a clunking hardline trajectory to death or glory.

Just *five* blocks away.

He saw some mole-like whisperers, hermetic and gloomy, holed up in otherwise uninhabited apartment complexes. They took in the sight of the old man with the unfinished suit of armor speckled in a slight patina, with the bewhiskered, slim face, the darting eyes, the hook-backed mare, the jug of sloshing water, the grocery bags; he was tired, an unconscionable fool, the epitome of a longshot. He didn't stand a chance. They sneered.

Four blocks.

He was amassing a greater following of gulls along with crows, a beaked envoy, who accompanied Don Miguel like flies to a corpse.

Three blocks.

He heard The Steel Dragon, maybe ten blocks away; maybe two, or five, or twenty-seven. He couldn't pinpoint the deathliness. It seemed everywhere, far, near, middle-distanced, quaking the streets, permeating the sky in sorrow.

Two blocks.

Don Miguel clutched his ram's horn, which he had tied to a flailing piece of pajama gown, then he blew into it, letting his cheeks balloon a ripe cherry-red, imbuing the 7th Avenue thoroughfare with his melody. It was the trumpet's song. It bellowed, it honked, while his trachea worked tiredly and his wind passages strained into tensile rope.

He heard the monster drawing nearer, screeching while crashing into buildings. So, he halted his awful bugling, and kicked his heels once more into the sides of his mare, galloping now, lowering his frame, letting the wind whip aerodynamically off their combined form. Don Miguel was becoming one with the animal.

Almost there.

Times Square was in his line of sight, resplendent with its phosphorescent billboards, its effulgent Golden Arches belying gluttony, its plastered super-sized Nikon advertisements, its palatial movie posters, its electric news ticker, its stock reports...... its STEEL DRAGON.

Times Square.

There it was, hovering, not zipping, but gliding ever so buoyantly in midair, about fifty to a hundred feet from the ground. The many faces of melted, mishmashed flesh glowered at Don Miguel from the coaster's back.

Seeing him skinny, and horse-bound, stopped within the sprawling junction of Broadway and 7th Avenue. He pointed his lance toward the Dragon, waggling it with a firm resolve.

"I'm here, dragon! It's time to die!"

The metallic beast, in response, brushed a course through the side of a building, burrowing a trough of shattered glass and pulverized mortar, then it paused, and it turned, and it floated, observing the bizarre little man.

All of the sixteen heads, encrusted like epidermal jewels within the demon's back, went from glowering to shrieking and hissing without sense.

"My name is Don Miguel Rigoberto de Ruiz and I have come to slay you, dragon. I expect you won't go down without a fight," he proclaimed, then trumpeted his ram's horn once more.

The Dragon, seemingly over the spectacle, went in, traveling at unconscionable speeds while the birds behind Don Miguel croaked and swam in circular flight patterns, a swarm of feathered locusts, and Don Miguel slunk himself into Rocinante, charging the deformity that charged him.

Weighing less than one one-hundredth of the rollercoaster, it was fortuitous that the beast missed him, crashing into the cement like a meteoric jackhammer, slowed, yet still burrowing through the ebony pavement, still moving forward.

Don Miguel pivoted his horse three hundred and sixty degrees. He charged, galloping along the coaster's left, climbing atop his horse, surfing her for a brief flicker of time, then faithfully jumping, landing on the Dragon.

The heads wailed. Wasting no time, Don Miguel began lancing them, letting the brains pop and spill out like cerebral pimples, fissuring the blemishes of intellect... making them spurt ectoplasmic ooze and slop and grey matter.

The remaining heads peered at Don Miguel, gnashing their already crumbling maws, clenching their eyes reflexively, trapped within the beast and yet possessed by it, comprising it. They howled and the coaster bucked, sending the old man aloft and away from the lurching freak.

He crashed, *hard*, onto the pavement.

By this time, his birds, his crows, his gulls, both laughing and sea, were already picking, pecking, and slurping, fattening themselves with the refuse of the punctured heads, while still swarming the flesh of the mutated faces that remained whole.

Don Miguel had unleashed a pungent, macabre aroma, like his roommate's rot-filled bedpan when he'd had colon cancer, when he bifurcated their skulls. He'd suspected the odor would be so awry, so off-putting, his wayward militia of scavengers would be drawn to it. They were.

The Steel Dragon wormed itself into an ascent, wriggling its train cars, trying to shake free and shoo the birds away. Blinded, as the birds smothered its deformed faces, forming a cloud of wings which flapped with synchronous thought, expanding and deflating, clawing and tearing away flesh with pincer-like talons.

The Dragon, with eleven of its heads remaining, however maimed, made some rickety, clangorous motions, streaming up and down like a monstrous eel on high, smashing itself into an advertisement of multiracial people drinking Diet Coke.

Distracted.

This bought Don Miguel some time. He was dazed and had a broken leg, but was barely scathed otherwise... Well, save for some cuts and purpling hematomas, and some dents in his armor and helmet.

His lance had flown from his hands, far, far away, and Rocinante was nowhere to be seen beneath the falling rubble.

He worked himself upright, putting most of his weight on one leg; he hopped, then fell, then crawled, while buildings rained down from above. Clambering once more into a standing position, he limped, dragging his broken leg over to his discarded lance. It'd fallen beside a sewer grating, a candy cane-colored TGI Friday's canopy, and a billboard for Discover cards.

Making it there, Don Miguel grabbed his lance, then whistled from pursed lips like a man whose ram's horn had been crushed a thousand times over. He saw Rocinante by a Hard Rock Café, snorting with fright, becoming bipedal every other second, standing on her haunches, with short bewildered jumps.

Her ears pricked at the sound of whistling, a sound somehow still audible through the wrecking noises produced by the Steel Dragon. Pivoting its head, making eye contact with the old man, Rocinante broke into a gallop, circumventing the fallen boulders and signs and crossing the street while evading death from above.

My girl. A horse like no other. A steed worthy of a true knight! thought Don Miguel, his chest swelling with pride as the clopping drew near. Reunited, Don Miguel gave his mare a swift pat on her snout, then bowleg-straddled the creature, whispering his praises, kicking his heels, then bending back down, dashing to mount yet another attack.

The Steel Dragon reeled, having lost four more of its heads, which left it with only seven. The deceased's eyes had been plucked out, allowing a viscous outpouring from the cranial openings, spewing thick blood, tendons, and bits of flesh.

The Dragon fought on, shaking the birds off like fleas, dragging its body over more billboards and buildings. It killed many in this way, reducing them to red streaks on battered facades. Then, it electro-screamed some others, sizzling them to a pulp of feathering talons.

The ones that remained swooped timidly, their enthusiasm dwindling as their brethren were killed.

Losing much of his aid, Don Miguel and Rocinante galloped closer still. So close that the old man made out the remaining faces, seeing them lacerated and moaning, their tongues lashing out like blood-filled sponges, their minds awash with confusion.

"I'm here, dragon," Don Miguel whispered.

He and his horse moved forward, confronting the monster on a messy strip of sidewalk. A battered Don Miguel smirked while holding his lance, and the otherworldly beast hesitated, slightly fearful in the unknowing, infuriated that the little man seemed a thousand feet tall, that his spirit grew and crested with daring gallantry and with honor. He had bested the leviathan, outsmarted the monster, beaten it back with equal measures of violence and wit.

Don Miguel glared at his tormenter with a brave, clear mind.

It stared back.

The Steel Dragon let its electro-shock fly from the unmoving mouth within the head of the rollercoaster. It sent the electricity forth in spidering currents that sliced through the dusty air.

A high-pitch ringing filled Don Miguel's skull and yellow exploded behind his eyes, as the wave enveloped him and Rocinante; his armor acting like a conduit and his lance a lightning rod. He lit up, bones flashing from beneath his epidermis, while his horse whinnied and screeched.

Don Miguel melted from the waist down, his armor melding to his flesh, his lance becoming fused with his hand. His lowermost appendages became intermixed and intermingled with Rocinante as both rider and horse convulsed and seized.

Their eyes sprung open as if lidless, as if the Ark of the Covenant were being shoved through their pupils, until Rocinante's head melted off and all that remained were the four knobby stems with hoofs, the hind and forelegs, and the horse's posterior, from its abdomen to its chest, and the armored human torso, arms, and head of Don Miguel.

He'd effectively become a centaur.

Huffing, not neighing, for he was still *himself*, still human, still an old codger, only mutated now from the mystified electrical stream, a current that'd turned him from person to creature, coalescing him into a beast.

Don Miguel steamed, his seared flesh a bruising vermillion, yet taut and sinewy, hellbent on vanquishing the demented thing that'd done this to him. He felt a new power, preternatural, primordial, surging in him, running through his flesh and horse fur, reinvigorating his human and his spliced animal half.

"My name is Don Miguel Rigoberto de Ruiz! And I have come to kill you, dragon!" he shouted with panache.

He began galloping, holding his lance up high as if he were heralding a crusade. The Dragon's heads mewled and the rollercoaster pounced down on its prey, who met the Dragon in midair, traveling at similar speeds.

Don Miguel flew, slicing through the metal face of the coaster and then all the way through its hull, dissecting it down the middle. The two incongruent halves went spiraling in different directions, slamming into the concrete and transforming it to softball-sized pieces of rubble.

Once divided, the Dragon flew no more.

Don Miguel, the freshly-baked centaur, drifted down to the two disparate halves, skewering the remaining heads, cracking them open like cans of red paint. He'd slain the Dragon. It was dead. He was a hero who could fly, and God only knew what else, but he couldn't open his right hand; it seemed irrevocably clenched and conjoined to his weapon.

DON MIGUEL FLEW home to Staten Island, specifically to Codger Life Estates. Strangely enough, the other residents didn't seem to notice much of a difference in his appearance. Or, if they did, they didn't let on.

"How do I look?" Don Miguel asked, galloping into the home's social area.

Most just shrugged.

Others clapped gently.

Some in the retirement home beamed.

They were just pleased to have their peculiar friend back. Most, who had the mental wherewithal, were proud.

The old man, their fellow tenant, had saved New York City.

A little later, his armor was surgically removed. Even the lance was sawed off, yet the metal-gauntleted hands were immovable. There was a period of healing, of convalescence, after which he lived quite comfortably. He did have a chronic pain in his back, a throbbing sensation he said stemmed from sleeping upright and vertical upon the body of Rocinante. It was his only complaint.

The days were uneventful, yet steady, consistently so. There were no more dragons to battle, no more metropolises to be rescued, no more civilizations skulking to faraway distances, hiding in dark recesses like subterranean voles.

He received accommodations, a key to New York City, wreaths and gift baskets aplenty, along with honorific ceremonies commemorating the day, that stupendous evening, when an 83-year-old centaur dispatched a mutant basilisk.

Don Miguel didn't dream. And he didn't believe himself to be Don Quixote, not anymore. He now knew that he was something entirely different, something unique, something just its own.

The revelation made him feel a sense of underlying peace, of contentment, knowing that he had slain his dragon, that he had fulfilled his personal destiny and had lived up to his own potential. A year later, on the anniversary of the Times Square Duel, Don Miguel the centaur died of old age, a smile riddling his wispy lips.

Hundreds upon thousands attended his funeral to pay their

debts, to keep something ignited within, to believe in something bigger, higher, better. They wept, for the innermost happenings of the soul resided in the higher planes of existence, far off from the earthly plateau and its hindrances. Yet, the old kook had demonstrated, elevation was possible.

Don Miguel Rigoberto de Ruiz was buried deeply in an oddly-shaped hole.

One that would not fit anyone.

Except for him.

TWO ROADS DIVERGED IN A WOOD...

The highway is much bleaker when you're dying. My wheels, they spun round and round and wore on the asphalt resembling a blackened tongue: unraveling for infinite distances, stretching to the edge of all things.

I'd been shot only once... in the side. Above the hip. I held the wound with one hand as blood spouted through my quaking digits. The sacks of money I'd robbed the bank for were in the back of a 1980 Ford Thunderbird I'd hijacked from a disco wimp.

Butter-yellow with a roof like hazel. Two-door. None of that four-door, family-faring excrement on wheels. It was a coup and a real one. I'd pistol-whipped him for it.

He had the rolled up-sleeves, and the white sports coat, and that weird jouncing bouffant, like some stand-in for Travolta, only softer.

He cried and I pistol-whipped him some more.

His face ruptured like a watermelon, all pinkish and reddish on the inside. I took his wallet, keys, and car, to flee to some nowhere town, hours and nights away, called Fairfield, in Nebraska. When I was there, I laid low. And soon, I resumed my life's purpose:

Of robbing banks

I'd had a good run of it, previously, but now, having dusted a security guard, who fucking shot me first, I might add, I was on the lam-lam. I'd never had so much heat on me. In fact, I could still see the red and blue wig-wags blaring hot in the distance in my rearview.

And it was there and then, on the bleak and onyx highway that I saw an off-road in the distance, grown over with grasses and brambles, but a road nonetheless. A way out, if they didn't see me turn onto it.

The road less taken looked untraversed for who knows how long. My only chance. So, I veered right, after cutting my headlights, of course, and bumped and jangled my way through the forest for a while. I couldn't see the piggish cops, yet I could hear the blur of their sirens as they zoomed past: ignorant of the fact that alls they were chasing was the air of an unfortunate night.

Soon, after some time going at a modest speed, voyaging by the light of a moon bloodshot like a malignant cyst, I turned my headlamps back on. The forest was a tangle of rotting branches, interwoven like a shawl of macabre mourning. And I felt I was in a one-man procession, the engine of the Ford Thunderbird singing me a private dirge as I awaited inevitable nothing.

There was still a road there. I was on it, asphalt overtaken with forest and earth, bumping as I clutched my side and hissed through my teeth. Nighttime beasties screeched solemnly and blinked bodiless and soon, the trees grew sparser, and the forest opened up to a clearing as I revved my engine and expelled myself from the inhospitable womb of the forest like a man rebirthed.

The road became smoother: less crisscrossed by overlapping slabs of asphalt, no longer overrun by thickened roots, potholes ceased to honeycomb my path. Beside me, on either side, corn stalks swayed with a nocturnal breath, primeval and uncaring. My foot was heavy that night. I didn't know where I was going, yet I knew I wanted to get far, far away.

I saw a farm coming up on my right hand side, and on its yard blazed a great pyre. As I sped closer, I could see signs, wooden and chipped, reading:

"EVERYTHING MUST GO!!" and "ESTATE SALE!!" and "TIME, IT TAKES ALL THINGS!!"

I drew nearer to the farmhouse and saw silhouettes of rusting grain silos rising up from the earth like swollen fingers. And I decelerated the Thunderbird before the sprawling yard-sale of dirt, seeing the plot was littered with mounds of garbage.

Floorboards and heaps of moldering dolls and teddy bears, broken-down rockers and shattered TV sets.

Also in the yard, lighted by the blaze of the inferno, stood a man: corpulent and hairless and completely nude. An overgrown baby, standing stock still with an overhanging gut, resembling a dermal balloon ready to *pop*.

Beside him, is what I took to be his wife: a scrawny crone hunched over and very naked too, with drooping, swaying breasts, protruding, gnarled nipples, and from what I could see, jutting vertebrae like huge pearls popping out of her skin.

Their eyes were hollow and listless.

They stared at me as I passed, genitals exposed and mouths panting, awful figures tickled by the orange crackling of their blaze. The smell was noxious. My head throbbed. My brain felt as though it were inflating, 'bout to crack open my skull.

For a moment, I forgot who I was or where I was. Forgot I had robbed the Pinnacle Bank. Forgot I had killed a man. Forgot I had a hole in my side. Forgot I was spurting blood.

All I could see was their grotesque form and figures. I became filled with an acute terror hitherto unknown. Odors redolent of sickbeds in hospices seeped through the cracks in my Thunderbird's windows.

I peeled out. Jammed my foot on the gas-throttle and got the hell out of there. The pyre was still raging and churning up smoke in my rearview. Those two, ill-born, mutant, whoever-they-weres gawked at me in the distance, with their eyes refracting light like anthracite coal.

Around me were expanses of whispering fields, serene under the watchful gaze of the moon. Or maybe, a big maybe, I was just leaking so much of my innards it seemed to be that way.

I kept driving. Thinking the cops of some jurisdiction or other were soon to catch on and soon to jam me up. I needed to get as far away as possible. Needed to lay low. Not so low I'm casketed underground, but low enough the heat would taper off and I could hopefully convalesce and not die fully. I already had one foot dipped in the other side.

Over there was a cold and icy place.

I tried not to think about the two naked fatheads barbecuing their belongings on a rotten heap. It was too bizarre. And too unsettling. Besides, I had more important things to worry about, for instance, the whop of a search copter's rotor over the trees from whence I emerged.

I could see the hemlocks flexing by the might of the copter's blades. A searchlight scanned the boughs and randomized bracken and the scattered starry-eyed wildlife that called the woods their home. The light went out over the fields of wheat and I kept speeding and it seemed to disappear.

No more dirigible was in sight. And soon, there was nothing more than darkness, with splashes of dehydrated evergreen trees on either side. I twisted-up my face, feeling drained of everything but a feeble wish to live.

Then, I heard the whop of the rotor again, or at least I thought I did, only it was terrestrial and was coming from a small gulch on the side of the road up ahead. I drove up tentatively, seeing a car turned on its side.

It was a weird-looking vehicle, with the tires still spinning lopsidedly and all banged-up as I slowed to a halt beside its mass. It grated a fresh moan, a live machine from the vaginal cogs and sprockets of some mechanical giantess... or assembly line.

When I drew closer, I could see, from its hood ornament, which was a platinum angel with whipped-back wings and outstretched arms holding some sort of disc, that its make was Packard... painted completely black with swooping and suave contours.

Its model was lost on me, but it seemed to be something from the Great Depression. An old-timey and beat-up whip that looked sort of new, besides its recent accident.

A man, dressed in a fine three-piece suit and battered fedora lunged from behind the old vehicle. He cradled a Thompson submachine gun in his arms and he said "fucking coppers" and started unloading rounds into my car and femur. Blood spurted over the white-leather interior.

The drum on his weapon rattled as he made a throaty chortle, like some sort of James Cagney in the original Scarface.

I lifted my Glock .45 pistol, and, while ducking my head, shot three or six times out of my passenger side window. I heard bullets ricocheting off metal, then some truncated *thuds*, like it'd bore its way into some human slabs of meat and his torrent of missiles stopped, so I slowly uncurled myself.

My mind was an unthinking mess, feeling filled with swabs of chloroform-soaked cotton.

I didn't know what was happening.

I painfully stepped out of my newly ruined luxury vehicle and dragged my bullet-ridden body around the perforated front of the car to see the man, the psychopath firing at me, slumped into the soil, leaning against his groaning Packard.

He was coughing up blood in bubbles and spurts. Glaring at me with eyes afire, bulging from his lean face.

The air swirled with scents of burnt rubber, twisted metal, and sentient corpses. I pressed my arm on my shot-side while my pistol applied pressure on my freshly wounded thigh, and I inched my way towards the maniac, who I could see, despite his state, was none other than the notorious Homer Van Meter.

Van Meter. The most ruthless and bloodthirsty member of John Dillinger's "Terror Gang." I studied bank robbers religiously as a kid. It's kind of how I got myself into this mess.

"Ye some kind of pistolero..." he coughed.

"Impossible..." I said.

"What's not possible is that you got the jump on me... for... for... a couple of banknotes? You'll be stuck at Alcatraz or dead in the ground very soon... just like the rest of us."

Marrow was gushing out of my leg like blood pudding, making the wound in my side old news for the moment. I couldn't believe I was looking at the man who gunned down police officers and plastic surgeons alike...

He'd tried to kill the doctor Wilhelm Loeser, when he was unhappy with the facial reconstructive surgery he received in his friend Jimmy Probasco's apartment.

Van Meter died in 1934, at the hands of four police officers, in a deluge of bullets that blew off most of his fingers. Now, this hatchet-faced ghoul with the puritanical stare was sputtering blood in my direction, blathering cliched platitudes.

"Who are you, really?"

"Someone who took you..." he coughed in a fit, "for a chump."

"What is this... what's going on?"

"Yer not going to take my money, that's what's going on..."

Van Meter attempted to raise his Tommy gun, but the drum and the whole mechanism seemed too heavy for him in the moment and I lifted my pistol and shot him in the face, cracking the back of his skull open like an old book.

Caterwauling, I wrested the Chicago typewriter from his limp hands and used it to shoot him dozens more times, coincidentally blowing off some of his fingers and making a mash of his frame.

I saw sacks of money, bloated and spilling green legal tender over their rims and I maneuvered best I could to them, and grabbed what I could, leaving a bag of cash behind.

I read about the four police officers who would take credit for killing Homer Van Meter. They reportedly found $1,323 dollars on the robber even though he supposedly stole ten thousand dollars that day. And now... I know why.

I fell into the driver's seat of my car, knowing I needed help soon, knowing I had to keep moving and stay awake best I could. I used the newly pilfered cash to plug the hole in my leg as I continued pressing down on my side and let the car chatter in a forward momentum.

The road was ebony and endless. There was no rotor whop and no heister from the Depression and no naked mongoloids burning their belongings. Just the road and the night stretching to the edge of all that was.

And it was that way, for a while.

Nothingness, just road and night, until I passed a cluttering of thirty or so wagons filled with strange settlers with starving eyes peering from under the white canvas covers, stretched so taut over the wagon beds of their filthy mobiles, and there were mothers clinging to sick and dying children.

They're just Quakers, I told myself, some off-the-grid band of religious zealots denouncing technology in all its forms. Even the Atari. Even the Walkman. The Thunderbird's headlights accentuated the pure filth and misery they must've been feeling, and I saw arrows protruding from some of the wagons making them look like battered porcupines trundling upon wobbling wooden spokes.

They gaped, all confused, as though I were not a dying man, but the angel of death hisself. A woman in a dusty bonnet clung to a toddler's contorted corpse, probably fell to cholera or the whooping cough or some other pilgriming disease, while wailing to the darkened sky about her suffering.

The person next to her, a bearded, defeated man, kept on mumbling, and I could hear him 'cause I was keeping pace and had blown out my passenger side window, that "time... it swallows all things," and that, "it runs into itself and starts the whole process over again."

And...

"This is just one of the many infinite lives we'll experience in the same exact way for all of eternity," and, "our suffering echoes through the cosmos and the fabric of existence itself. Our hurt is a scar, a stain, a mother's cries permanently mutate the circle we're doomed to never stop traversing," or something like that.

It seemed as though they'd been on the demented Oregon trail for uncounted millennia. I knew my mind was playing tricks. And I was surely dying. And I'd lost a lot of blood. I was probably delusional and seeing mirages, like in a desert, only it was a frigid Nebraska highway traversed by only me and the earth's oddest performers.

As I was driving, my brain, which I figured my whole life to be some sort of computer, was shutting off. I kept throttling towards salvation of some kind not knowing where the highway, that bent and turned only ever so slightly, went.

And it wasn't until I saw an enormous mass of wetted fur on the side of the road in my headlights that I slowed the Thunderbird once more. I drove up on it, this majestic heft, and my car creaked in its forward motion.

I was staring at roadkill, the likes and size of which were impossible.

Hazel furs swayed every which way in the creeping wind, wiry and elongated and sticking out of a hide that shouldn't be in a ditch in the boondocks. Van Meter shouldn't have either, but... this was an even weirder sight.

I put the Thunderbird in park with the headlamps still gleaming over towards the dead animal, lighting its immensity so I could know what I was looking at. And I limped and hobbled towards the road-kill... the smell nearly knocked me unconscious.

It had been putrefying for some time, seemingly from the inside out.

A light snow began to drift down in floating motes and I saw the snowflakes land on my shoulders and trembling hands and the forever-road and the rotted leviathan. Then the snow melted, as soon as it touched down. Just puddled and disappeared. Here. Then never was.

I crept closer, breathing clouds of cold air and the snow melted on the animal's fur and I could see its legs like stout pillars and its fur draping over a ribcage that stuck out from its body. The roadkill had tusks.

Large and curving, bigger than my vehicle. Its trunk curled out from its face like an auburn anaconda. I couldn't believe it. I just stared. It was a wooly mammoth.

Maybe the last of its kind? Just dead and rotting beside this middle-of-nowhere stretch of asphalt and it seemed so alone, and I felt so lonesome and lost looking at it. I hadn't cried in some time, but as I held my side and my leg and looked around for anyone who

could help, and screamed, even for the fucking cops, I knew I was
done for.

If that hallowed pachyderm couldn't survive in this world, why
should I? How could I? I dragged myself back to the Thunderbird and
fell back into the car shaking. I closed the door and drove off once
more, looking at the wooly mammoth as I passed.

I thought I'd seen the strangest of all things, but I drove and drove
and the world around me swirled as I gunned it past what looked like
a band of Neanderthals, all beetle-browed and stubby, wearing furs
and carrying spears, and then later, hours maybe, the forest around
became a wild tangle, so lush and liberated.

My eyelids grew heavy... I witnessed huge condors fly near the
setting sun and my world changed when I saw the silhouette of a
brontosaurus' neck and head craning out over the trees.

The landscape transmogrified as the dial on the Thunderbird's
speedometer strained to the right, and my gas evaporated into the
roaring vehicle, and bills loosened and flitted through the car's blood-
splotched interior.

The animals grew smaller until there weren't any left and I drove
and drove until the long highway that stretched to the edge of all
things eventually ended at a beach and I was staring at the ocean.

Its waves shouldering up the sky and spraying a white foam as
they crashed in upon themselves.

It was the most beautiful thing I'd ever laid eyes on and I don't
think I'd ever felt such a strange peace like being home as the Thunderbird slowly crept over the sand and I submerged itself in the
prehistoric salt water that poured in through the open passenger side
window.

I leaned back, kept my foot on the throttle and let the ocean take
me, my money, my sins. Hell, I was about to die anyway... so I smiled
widely as the water rose over my head and everything turned night
again. Complete darkness, besides a speck of immense multicolor up
ahead that might best be described as a singularity, ready to burst
and to start it all over again...

I drove into it and found that time... really does swallow all things.

I shall be telling this with a sigh
Somewhere ages and ages hence:
Two roads diverged in a wood, and I—
I took the one less traveled by,
And that has made all the difference.

— **Robert Frost**

JUST MILLIMETERS DEEP

Walter leaned closer to the mirror, stretching his body over the bathroom sink. He ran his trembling fingers through his brown hair.

Am I imagining it? No! My hair is thinning. My skin is thinning. I'm touching my skull!

He was, *indeed*, touching his skull!

The truth was undeniable. There it was, reflected before him. Where, just yesterday, a healthy quaff of well-conditioned hair lay—now, there was nothing but retreating flesh.

He touched it again. Probed and hissed. The skull shone bright white, in sharp contrast to his tanned skin and the remaining auburn swoop of his hairline.

"How! How!?" Walter beseeched the mirror, gritting his teeth.

Why is this happening? Not today.

Not as he readied himself for dinner with his fiancée, Yui, and her father, Katsu Yakimoto (owner of Yakimoto Jewelers, the biggest jewelry chain in South Bend, Indiana).

With his well-trimmed fingernail, Walter tapped at the swath of skull, making a *click, click, clicking* noise.

This was the night, over finely seared steaks, and side salads, that they would tell Katsu of their engagement. Katsu, who was also Walter's boss, would only begrudgingly approve of the marriage.

What were his chances now, with a softball-colored skull overtaking his hairline?

Wincing, he fiddled with the knot of his tie, checked the press of his dress shirt's collar and reinspected his suit jacket. They all looked fine. Impeccable, even. Just as his clothes always were. Pristine and pressed and expensive.

But that piece of skull—that pesky piece of skull. It glowered like the mad eye of a cyclops. And beneath the piece of skull, his face looked terrible.

It seemed loose, like an anorexic's sweater. Bags hung under his eyes; purple bags that weren't present the day before.

Walter pushed at his cheeks, up and down and up again. They drooped; they sagged. It may be undetectable to most, but he noticed, and that's what counted. Would his fiancée notice?

He had tried so hard to make something of himself. Tried so hard to be *successful*.

Toiling in jewelry store after jewelry store—peddling wedding bands of differing karats, diamond studded earrings, and white gold pendants for over a decade—Walter hoped to triumph over an unpleasant upbringing.

Raised by a single father, Walter Sr., a slovenly man who reeked of dust and body odor, who hoarded ephemera and obscure bric-a-brac; a man more interested in his outdated books than the things of this world. It was a wonder Walter Jr. made it out semi-unscathed.

It was a wonder...

And ten years ago, he'd gotten his first jewelry store job, and he made it a point to dress better than his father, and to practice good hygiene, and he tried to be engaged in the world.

He'd been proud of himself, proud that his ambition had created results, even if his father didn't care or show any interest in his achievements. Even if Walter Sr. didn't show any interest in his namesake's life.

It didn't matter.

Walter cared about himself. Walter showed an interest. And Walter had worked so, damned, hard.

Rubbing his eyes till they turned a blemished scarlet, he gazed back into the mirror. His skull was still showing.

He thought back to his time at the jewelry store. Thought back to his trajectory from then, until now, to this horrific and solitary moment he found himself in.

Katsu, who usually grunted at Walter in lieu of speaking, tolerated him for his mere competence. And when he wooed Yui, who was ten years his junior, Katsu seemed to ignore the courtship—a tacit, yet detached form of approval.

With the white bone winking under the bathroom lights, Walter shuddered, scared the patch of skull foreshadowed something much worse. He barely recognized himself now.

Is this aging? It has to be... there's no other explanation for it. I'll go to the hospital tomorrow. I'll go if it's still there.

Walter looked older, so much older than he did the day before, when he was vibrant and sporty, so much older than his thirty-three years.

He imagined agedness pursuing like a panther, stalking its quarry from thick, tropical boughs, taking occasional swipes with its razor-sharp claws.

He checked his suit one more time, still perfect. He stared at the bare patch of skull, still hauntingly there. He grabbed some bandages from under the sink and began dressing the opening. It didn't hurt, so he could barely call it a wound.

Applying gauze and medical tape, Walter redoubled his determination to garner Katsu's approval. One day, he'd be in charge of his own jewelry store. One day, he'd be *something,* unlike his father.

WALTER STRODE into Big Angus's Hibachi Steakhouse with an air of false confidence. Rubbing his open palms against his suit, he glanced

three times at his reflection in the lobby's window—paying particular attention to the bandage—and approached the hostess.

Her overworked eyes were strained with mascara and she stood next to a traditional Japanese-style door: a wooden lattice with translucent white sheets of paper filling the spaces between the wooden squares.

"I'm here for Yakimoto... party of three," Walter said with an empty smile.

The hostess nodded and studied a heavily inked form on the podium before her. She nodded again, spoke into a small walkie talkie pinned to her shirt, and said, "Right this way, Mr. Ellis. Your party has already been seated, but they're expecting you."

Walter checked his fancy gold watch, inlaid with sterling silver. He was thirteen minutes late. Sweat dewed his temples.

He followed the hostess as she slid the wood and paper room divider open, revealing the sizzling soy sauce-drenched world within. Walter noticed them immediately. Waiting.

Sitting at the far end of the restaurant, Mr. Yakimoto and his daughter shifted in their seats. A frown stretched and stretched, like a long gash, across the lower portion of his boss's face.

"Every zeptosecond holds great import. Every fraction of a moment can be spent calculating more ways to accrue wealth," Walter remembered Mr. Yakimoto saying.

He'd told him this on his first day of work. He'd also told it to him two days ago, when he was making the usual rounds visiting all of the stores in his chain. He said it, or something similar, almost every day.

Shit, why did I leave him waiting... Walter thought, his throat tightening, his extremities tingling, his blood running cold.

Approaching, Walter noticed the imposing, freakish width of Yakimoto. His shoulders were like the two escarpments of a cliff, on top of which loomed a monument in the form of an uber-serious face shrouded in ebony and silver hair.

He decided to focus on Yui, all made up and innocent. Virginal, even, although he knew she wasn't, with an attractive shock of black hair trimmed cutely to the midpoint of her neck.

Walter felt the slickness of sweat start to trickle from his armpits. This place was a zoo.

Shrimp and small slices of seared skirt steak were being flung through the air by hibachi chefs in tall white hats. Heavy, joyous diners wrapped around their respective grills, cheering, clapping their palms together like circus seals addicted to yum-yum sauce.

They tried their best to catch the food—their mouths open, their chins tilted toward the ceiling.

A hunk of steak was tossed, only to strike a toddler in the eye.

Walter gently prodded his bandage. It was still there, still covering his skull. A shrimp whizzed in front of him and struck his polished shoe. It made a wet, slapping sound.

He barely noticed.

Preoccupation enveloped Walter like a suffocating cloud as he followed the impertinent hostess who seemed less human than he.

Walking... walking... His feet felt like they belonged to someone or *something* else. A bird perhaps, since they seemed composed entirely of hollow bones, fragile and untrustworthy.

He wished he could be anywhere but here. Under his covers, begging any god who would listen to return the skin on his head.

The dim lighting of the restaurant lent a dreamlike, nightmarish quality to the whole venue. Finally, Yui spotted him. She gawped worriedly as he wove his way between the restaurant's many patrons.

I'm so fucking late, Walter thought, his stress mounting, thrumming in his glands with every ticking second. He began muttering under his breath:

"It's my skull... it's showing... you have to understand... no... I can't tell them... no way... how did this happen... I must've lost track of time in the..."

"Here you are, sir," interjected the hostess, pulling Walter's seat out from under the table.

Here I am.

Swallowing, Walter felt something akin to iron wool scrape a course down his throat. He took his seat and opened his mouth, but before he could say a word, Mr. Yakimoto folded his arms and spoke.

"You're late."

"Yes, Mr. Yakimoto, I'm sorry I—"

"Our time is precious, Walter. I hope you wouldn't treat customers with the same discourtesy."

"N-no, I'm sorry Mr. Yakimoto. Just hit my head on the way out. I'm just clumsy, I..."

Walter watched the older man flare his nostrils, as if sniffing the lie. He then watched Yui's eyes widen with genuine concern.

"Oh my God, your head!" she squeaked. "What happened?"

"I slipped in the kitchen. Yeah, um. I don't know how it happened. There must've been a leak from the roof, or maybe the sink."

Mr. Yakimoto tilted his head, inquiring. He crossed his arms and placed them on the table.

"Yeah! I whacked my forehead on the corner of the stove. Blood spurted everywhere. It was terrible. I even went unconscious for a few minutes."

Mr. Yakimoto's pointer finger jumped up and down on his emerald cufflink. Sneering, he was lost in a world just his own, a world of judgment. A world of coldhearted decision making.

"So... I'm really sorry I'm late. I would never keep you both waiting. Not purposefully, that is."

Walter gave his best attempt at a charming grin. Unlike any other day, it felt strained and insecure.

Where's my mojo? Where's my salesmanship when I really need it!? The heat in the restaurant made Walter's head wobble, he felt the warmth creeping beneath his flesh, untethering his skin from his bones.

"Are you still hurt?" asked Yui. "You seem so... pale."

"I'm alright. Just a bad spill, really."

"You do look very pale, Walter. Very unwell. Are you sure you're ok?" asked Mr. Yakimoto.

"Yes, completely fine, sir. As I said, I just banged my head. Nothing to worry about, really."

Mr. Yakimoto leaned back in his chair. A synthetic look of concern played about his stiff features. Walter's heart began thudding fast and arrhythmic under his sternum. He shifted his focus to Yui. She glared at him in a way he'd never seen before.

"Did you cut your hair?" she asked.

"Um... no. What do you mean?"

"It looks thinner in some ways. Like brittle or... I don't know. It's all on the shoulders of your jacket. Are you sure you're ok?"

Walter was not his usual smooth self. He awkwardly pushed his chin into his throat to sneak a glimpse of his body. And Yui was right. Thin strands of hair lay meekly tangled on his suit's shoulders.

I'm losing my hair! Fuck! Is more of my skull showing!

Walter clasped his hands under the table. They squirmed like a pair of frigid, half-dead cod. They were cold. Colder than normal.

"It's... uh... yeah... I... I'm sorry I'm really not feeling too great..."

"Excuse me, are you on drugs?" Mr. Yakimoto squinted.

"Of course not, no!"

"So, you're ok to eat? Even with your graying skin?" Mr. Yakimoto lifted his eyebrow, quizzically.

"Graying skin?"

Yui and her father sat and beheld Walter in rapt silence. Mr.Yakimoto let his face settle once more into a stoic, stonelike expression.

You never liked me, did you? You just think I'm a white dork with no real family. You just put up with me because I'm good at my job.

"I've already ordered your meal for you, Walter, but you look like death itself. Do you need to leave?" said Mr. Yakimoto.

"I... I... don't really know what's going on." Walter glanced at his hands.

A long strip of sinewy flesh and muscle swung limply from his left palm, exposing the jointed bones beneath. He didn't even feel it; didn't even detect the skin coming off.

Horrified, Walter watched as streams of sangria-colored blood dripped onto the carpet of the hibachi grill. Then he felt a chill seize his spine.

"How..." he mumbled.

Just then, the hibachi chef arrived at their private table: six-feet tall, not counting his chef hat, and fresh faced with an entertainer's demeanor.

"Hello, hello, hello," he said, bowing slightly with every greeting.

He started clanging a metal spatula and a large two-pronged fork on the grill in front of him, swaying back and forth as he did so. Lifting a white-sleeved arm, he twirled the spatula around and around on top of the fork 'till it blurred.

An impressive feat, but everyone's attention was elsewhere.

Walter couldn't stop glaring at his palm and the bones—and he couldn't stop shaking. Mr. Yakimoto, in a fit of frustration, leaned his wide-shouldered body forward to speak.

"I know you were going to announce your engagement. I am not naïve, Walter. But, if you are on drugs or you're drunk, which is very disappointing, *I MIGHT ADD*, then you have no place at Yakimoto Jewelers and you have no place with my daughter!"

"Sir... I..."

The hibachi chef created a tall conical structure with sliced white onions and, pouring some sort of flammable liquid into its core, caused a spurt of flame to shoot from its top, like a volcano.

"Yea! Yea!" the chef said and scanned the table. No one was watching.

Tears began forming in the ducts of Yui's big hazel eyes. Walter let her down, and he couldn't think of the right words to fix it. She began to cry. A soft whimper first, then a full flood of tears.

"I'm sorry. I'm really sorry." Walter said, watching Yui's slender frame bounce as she sobbed. He hated seeing her upset. That, and Walter's deadbeat father, were actually the two things he hated seeing most.

Mr. Yakimoto leered. "So, you are sick?"

"Yes! Mr. Yakimoto... I'm really unwell. If you'll please excuse me this one time... and I'm really sorry, Yui, I didn't mean for dinner to go this way."

The hibachi chef made a heart with fried rice. He slid his metal spatula under its center and tapped the handle to make it seem as

though the heart were beating. He did this for about four *thuds.*
Then, he turned his spatula on its side, making the heart split in two.

"You have work tomorrow, don't you, Walter?"

"Yes, sir, and if you don't mind, I might need to take the day off.
This head injury... it might be worse than I'd thought."

Mr. Yakimoto touched the full Windsor knot of his tie, grunted,
and looked at his crying daughter.

"You wouldn't want to disappoint us, Walter. I ask you to tread
lightly. Figure out whatever it is you've got going on because I expect
you to be at work the day after tomorrow, no exceptions!" Mr. Yakimoto slammed his fist onto the table.

Walter nodded, feeling the skin on the back of his neck stretch
taut as he did so. He wanted to embrace Yui. Wanted to say something
to ease her sorrow. But he couldn't, not in front of her father.

"I'll call you tomorrow, Yui," he said, still nodding, feeling the skin
on the back of his neck *tear* ever so slightly; still feeling the dark
blood *drip, drip, dripping* from his palm.

Yui wouldn't look up. She buried her head in her father's chest
and he patted her back and shook his head.

"Shape up! If you are sick, then I hope you feel better *very* soon. If
you aren't, then there's no place at Yakimoto Jewelers for addicts or
drunks!"

"I'm just unwell. The whole head thing, I promise... I'm very sorry
about this, sir. And Yui, I'm so sorry... I have to go..."

Walter rose from the table, nodding still, concealing his palm by
pressing it against his stomach then covering it with his good hand.

Half observing his fiancée and her bobbing shoulders, half
avoiding Mr. Yakimoto's frigid stare, he hurried away, nearly plowing
through the hostess and a group of simpering twenty-somethings.

After rushing into the parking lot, he doubled over and puked.

He then stumbled his way to his blue Saab sedan, shut himself
inside of it, and began to sob.

What in the fuck is going on?

Fumbling with his rearview mirror, he turned it so he could see
his reflection. A gaunt, grayish face stared back at him. With watery,

bloodshot eyes like gelatinous ping-pong balls, and sagging cheeks, and lips that were an eggplant purple.

"FUCK! I look like a god damned ghoul!" Walter screamed.

He touched the back of his neck, and feeling the sharp knobs of three fully exposed vertebrae, he wailed again.

SITTING on the ornate Persian carpet in his apartment's living room, rocking at a frenetic pace, Walter told himself that it was all a nightmare, or the result of food poisoning, or the aftermath of an LSD drugging that he wasn't privy to.

"That's it!" he said. "A barista slipped something into my coffee this morning. Yeah! That has to be it!"

He touched the back of his neck again, feeling the cold, wet contours of his C3, C4, and C5 vertebrae. All he could think of were skinless grapes, covered in a tangle of nerves. Fingering the nerves, back and forth, and back and forth, his mind racing, he eventually felt them *snap*, sending waves of pain through his body.

He stopped rubbing.

Lifting himself upright, Walter marched his way to his restroom so he could fully inspect himself in the mirror once more. Shock, stupefaction, and terror waited.

He'd lost more of his hair, and more of his skull now showed; his skin having eroded further past the scope of the bandage.

"Definitely on drugs. No doubt it's drugs. I'm on drugs..."

Walter carefully peeled the bandage off, fully exposing the bone beneath. The stark-white curvature of his skull distinguished itself in the mirror, especially when compared to his diseased-looking face, its skin running like wet sand.

He decided to study his palm again. The hole was still present; still jagged; still deep.

The bones moved, one on top of the other, like well-oiled joints.

For a moment, Walter forgot to be horrified, experiencing a morbid sort of intrigue.

Why am I not bleeding more? he wondered, noticing the blood he did have exited his body thick and coagulated, as though mixed with dirt.

I could stare at myself all night, but the drugs will still be in me. Just sleep it off... Just sleep it off. Tomorrow, I'll call Yui and straighten every-thing out. My life's on track... it still is.

Walter, holes and all, shuffled into his bedroom, flicked the lights off, and crawled under his covers. Being exhausted, he drifted into a deep sleep.

WALTER DREAMT of a mother he'd never known. A mother, beautiful, brunette, affectionate, nurturing, who allegedly died of colon cancer when he was three.

She stood waist high, just offshore of a tumultuous ocean as waves crashed down and down upon her young frame. Somehow, she remained standing with her arms spread wide, wide-eyed staring toward her son on the beach, begging for her life.

"Mom! Mom! I'm coming!" Walter shouted.

But she didn't answer, only shrieked, as more and more waves came.

In a fit, Walter rushed from the shoreline, waded in, and dove face-first into the omnipresent blue-blackness of the ocean. He paddled out doing freestyle strokes, but the waters grew deeper, and the waves bigger, and his mother seemed further and further away.

No. Just keep going. It'll be different. Just hold on!

Swimming like a man possessed, Walter started to near his mom who'd been brought out further by the currents, until he was just a few feet away, and he swam, bringing his arms overhead, ignoring the burning, piercing sensation in his lungs, and he could almost touch her... His hand reaching out, the fingers trembling as they brushed her clothes.

"I've got you!"

Walter felt like a little boy again, felt like a child who'd just overcome their personal monster.

And then, his mother vanished, and that little boy found himself adrift in the middle of the storming waters. He gasped for air between tsunamis, but couldn't hold his breath since the waves had grown too big, too awesome in their force.

Helpless, he watched the dark-shimmering waters crest overhead. Then, the waves crumbled down like so many liquid stones.

Mouth open, his body was filled, becoming a decanter of seawater and spume.

Then, he revolved and wailed, plummeting into a great abyss of utter darkness. No longer in an ocean, but in a limbo between beingness and nothingness.

He plunged into the onyx void until his consciousness shifted, and he became the surrounding darkness perceiving the fall of a human figure.

He became the shadow. The night. Beholding the flickering fleetingness of life.

A few hours later, Walter woke up.

HIS EYELIDS HAD THINNED in his sleep, till they were sheets of parchment paper barely shielding the morning light filtering through his windows. Being sensitive to any light while sleeping, Walter was jarred awake.

"No..." he groaned. "Was it? A nightmare?"

Walter's tongue lolled, rubbing against a parched inner cheek. It too, had the feeling of thinness, like a cannoli slurped of its creamy innards. He rolled to his side and as he did so, he felt something peel from his back. A cold wind gripped him, along with jolts of sharp pain.

It's just the bedsheet. Must've stuck to my skin. Maybe I was sweating?

Walter often did sweat while asleep, especially during the summer, and especially when anxieties pressed upon his mind. *It was the body's way of purging its stresses*, he thought.

Even as aches thrummed through his joints, he *was* becoming more and more alert, so he thought his whole experience of yesterday was a dream, or, as he had wholeheartedly posited, an acid trip.

"That dinner couldn't have gone any worse," he muttered.

He thought back on all the awkward, awful moments that seemed to come, one after the other, in a parade of disappointment. Walter's pulse quickened.

"*Noooo!*" he muttered a second time, still in bed.

The bad memories were the perfect motivation to move. Walter swung his feet onto his bedside carpet, feeling the skin on the back of his calves peel off the bedspread as he did so.

His butt cheeks also stuck, tapelike, as he rolled upright and to his feet. Suddenly, his thin eyelids rocketed back, spring-loaded on his surprise.

Walter's bed was covered in skin and muscle and sinew. The shape of a person's back and glutes and triceps and calves and heels. It took Walter a second to realize that they were *his own*.

Too scared to scream, Walter lurched into his restroom once more. A foreign face glared back at him in the mirror. It did not seem his own, because it was barely even there.

His countenance hung like loose rags, sallow, turning to ash. He pressed a quaking finger to his cheek. It ripped under the slight pressure. He touched his neck, feeling the vertebrae still protruding from the night before. He checked his hand, peering at the bones inside of his wrist.

Walter spun 'round and glanced over his thinned shoulder. He saw his spinal column, ribcage, lungs, shoulder blades, all laid bare. All missing that sheath of flesh that is just millimeters deep.

Dropping his pants, he looked at his penis.

Now, Walter could scream.

AT FIRST, it was like any other early afternoon at the jewelry store on West Sample Street. The occasional customer would come in to purchase or resize a wedding band. An elderly member of the gentry might stop by to ogle some pearls. Young couples strolled in, arms slung across each others' hips, to chuckle at prices they couldn't afford.

The day moved slow like melting glass. And the air outside was stagnant and still. Then a peculiar man walked in, wearing a manilla trench coat, sunglasses, a baseball cap, his face and hands swathed in bandages. He looked like a contemporary version of H.G. Wells' *The Invisible Man*.

He scanned the store and trundled forth, passing by casing after casing of watches and pendants and sapphire rings. Reaching the cash register, he stood in front of a stubby woman with a beehive hairdo, glasses, and pink lipstick: Claire.

"Is Yui here?"

"Is that you... Walter?" she stammered.

"Listen," he said, voice gruff. "I need to speak with Yui."

"Well, she's in the back right now." Claire's eyes were magnified behind her Coke bottle lenses. Trepidation turned her pale.

"It's really important. Can you get her now, please?"

"What happened? Is everything ok?"

"No! It's not *OK*, Claire, now please get Yui!"

A few elderly customers glanced toward the register.

Claire, who worked under Walter, so she had to obey, nodded nervously and shimmied off, moving like a gerbil whose cage had been rattled. All was not well at this particular Yakimoto Jewelers.

After some hushed speaking, Yui emerged from the back of the jewelry store. Her face twisted in anger, then a worried look settled her features. She seemed puzzled as she strode, and came around the register, inching up to Walter.

"Walter, why are you dressed like that? Did you get in an accident!?" she whispered.

"Can we go to the alley behind the store? I need to talk to you, but I can't in front of all these people."

Clutching her pearls, Claire peeped her big hair, thick spectacles, tiny mouth and all from behind a matte gray filing cabinet. Elsewhere in the store, the elderly couple clucked at one another, trying to decide if this costumed man was a pervert readying himself for some inevitable exposure.

"Yeah, of course, let's go," Yui nodded.

Side by side, the pair walked through the store while Yui assured the customers that all was well. She just needed to speak with her *friend* for a moment.

"You know how hair can thin, you know, as we get older?"

"Yeah, but your hair's always been so nice."

"I know. I know. But... what I want to say, like the thinning of hair, my skin's thinning too..."

"Huh?" Yui's eyes grew to the size of saucers.

"Please don't yell when I show you this, Yui. I'm really *fucking scared* right now and I don't have anywhere else to go."

Walter began pulling the sleeve of his coat back, inch by inch. Hissing, while shocks of pain coursed through his nervous system. He breathed erratic breaths and his paper-thin nostrils sucked against his septum, then billowed out again like windblown sails.

Yui let out a high screech.

She saw the elongated ligaments and muscles exposed and fraying and seeping an oily-black blood. They were flanked by the ulna and radius bones of the forearm, which crested like skinny white whales through the surface of a gore-ridden sea.

Yui stumbled rearward, wobbling, howling. Walter tried to reach out and catch her, but, reflexively, she squirmed, scratching at the bandages on Walter's face, tearing them off.

She shrieked again.

Not a face, but a skull with bugging eyes, chattering teeth and strips of dangling, decaying flesh stared back at her.

"Yui, please!! I tried to explain!! Please don't be frightened, I need you!! Please don't yell..."

Falling over, then scrambling upright, Yui hastened her way from the alley behind Yakimoto Jewelers.

"Wait! Yui! Please!! I'm begging you, please!!" Walter crowed.

But she wouldn't listen. She was gone. Long gone. And the truth of that fact stung worse than any of Walter's disintegrating nerve endings. He found himself staggering there, alone in the alley, faced with a new conundrum.

The piping, piercing, blood-curdling shrillness of Yui's screams had attracted a small crowd.

A group of citizens, with questioning expressions, looked on as the very haggard man stalked the howling woman. It seemed that he was lunging as the woman was shrieking, and screeching, and flailing for her escape—blowing past the onlookers and back into the jewelry store.

"Hey, asshole!" yelled a man in a sleeveless denim vest. "The hell you think you're doing! You stay right there, or I'll kick your fuckin' ass!"

Other members of the group cheered for the guy, offering their support. A labored, whining wheeze left Walter's tattered throat as he turned to face his audience.

The crowd stepped back. A woman fainted. Another man began chanting *El diablo! El diablo!* over and over again. The tough guy was at a loss for words. His lips trembled, and he stuttered, becoming incapacitated with shock.

"WHAT CAN YOU DO TO ME THAT'S WORSE THAN THIS!!" Walter screamed. And so did the crowd.

They scattered in every direction while Walter lurched forward and blundered his way down the street. He fell into his blue Saab sedan, and, unable to cry, for his tear ducts had long left him, Walter let out a long, anguished croak.

Turning the key in his ignition with a disintegrating hand, he shifted gears, then sped off to the only person that might have answers, the only person who could possibly help him. The man he hated most.

His father.

WALTER HADN'T SEEN his father in nearly twenty years. He left when he was fifteen, and his dad didn't seem to care enough to notice. Even when he lived on the streets for a short while, it was a welcomed respite when compared to the sheer discomfort of his childhood home.

After hours on the road spent losing his ears and much of the skin on his arms, torso, and legs, Walter saw the house.

It seemed like more of a crypt, composed of moldering grey bricks, than someone's home. Bones chittering, Walter took his foot off the gas. Unpleasant memories washed through the still-present connections in his brain.

He parked and got out and trundled to the door, stamping over a dead lawn whose only life rested in a smattering of weeds. A faded political sign for Ross Perot jutted at a slant to its side, rotting, just like him.

Abutting the sign was Walter's childhood tricycle. Once cherry red, now penny-colored with rust. It should've been in a trash heap, along with his crumbling body. Walter rattled his skeletal hand against the chipping door. Banged and banged and banged until he heard a shuffling from within.

Suddenly, a light cut on.

The door creaked wide and Walter gaped at the man he'd hated for as long as he could hate. There he was, swaying in his dingy sweatpants, rubbing his grimy hand on his sweat-stained undershirt, touching the crusty yellow spectacles tottering on the end of his round, ruby nose.

His father was plump, unwashed, and unshaven. A dirty man's stubble festooned his stinking face, and a crown of wispy hairs hung like thin filaments from his sick head.

Walter stood, flabbergasted. It was possible that his father looked worse than even he. For a moment, he forgot his situation, and instead pondered his dad's resemblance to a homeless Benjamin Franklin.

"Yes?" asked Walter Sr. Somehow, not reacting to the half-skeleton that stood before him.

"It's me, your son..."

Walter's father squinted and touched his glasses and rubbed his stomach.

"I thought this might happen someday," he said, without feeling. "Come in. I'll brew us a pot of coffee."

Walter Sr. turned on his heels and waved over his shoulder as though he was greeting someone he saw on a regular basis—not his long-lost son; a son who was quickly ripening to bones.

Walter wanted to leave, but he had no choice and nowhere else to go. So, he stepped into the crypt-like home he grew up in.

A sour stench assaulted the hole in the middle of Walter's face. It was as though decomposing fruits and feces had been left to mature under chairs and unseen niches around the house. Thin flaps of skin around his nasal aperture fluttered as he began hyperventilating.

The place existed as he remembered it: a dump. Yellowing news-papers and obscure anatomy and medical books were stacked head-high beside a heavily indented, legless couch.

Old photos hung askew, covered in dust on the walls. Everything was bathed in a dirty flypaper-colored light, possibly because the place was so filthy, or possibly because Walter Sr. liked and bought the bulbs dim.

Walter moved, following his dad into the modest kitchen with the crusted tiles and the mountains of dirty plates. The old Frigidaire looked like it had been soaked in urine. The curtains were stained from cigarette smoke, and a random assortment of insects laid belly up wherever the eye wandered.

Walter couldn't take it anymore, his panic turned into a shaking rage, and he screamed.

"What's happening to me!? What do you mean this might happen —some..." Walter's voice faltered, becoming hoarse and low.

"What's happening, dad, please..."

Walter Sr. nodded and returned with two dirty cups of coffee. He plopped down and ruminated on his son's question for a while, studying the sorry state his offspring found himself in.

"Can you take off your shirt, please?" he asked.

Walter blinked. His eyelids had become translucent, and they were going... going... gone.

"Why?"

"I need to see the progression. I need to see how far you've deteriorated."

With skinless fingers, Walter began unbuttoning his shirt until he laid his torso bare. His ribcage curled around his slippery, squelching organs as his bright white sternum, knobbed and ridged, contrasted the sallow surroundings of the room.

Naked, dangled Walter's heart, beating below his chest cavity, while his intestines lay coiled by his garbling stomach in the seat of his pelvis.

Walter Sr. studied the scene with detached coldness. He squinted and took a sip of his coffee.

"I can't help you," he said.

"What do you mean..."

"I can only explain to you why you're like this. And to be frank, it's a wonder you've made it this far."

Walter looked down at his forearms and hands. All of his skin had left him. The tendons seemed to be thinning, eroding, and leaving, too.

"*Tell me...*" he said.

"Your mother didn't die of colon cancer when you were three years old. She died before your birth. And before you say anything, don't. Because this is a semi-long story, and you don't have much time left."

Walter Sr. pushed the steaming coffee to his son, who ogled it with his protruding, lidless eyes.

"I thought your mother to be a beautiful specimen. She really was the most splendid woman I had ever laid eyes upon. But I knew she would never have me. Would never accept someone like myself. For I'm an ugly man." Walter Sr. gestured to his mirthless face—the prime example in his macabre show and tell.

"So, I waited for her—waited as she left her job at the florist; watched her from some bushes as she locked up. Women really shouldn't walk alone at night.

"Suffice it to say, I followed her, and I waited until she meandered in between the lighted places and I struck her down and murdered her. I promise you, she died pretty swiftly, and didn't struggle much."

Walter Jr., enraged, tried his best to stand up. But his thigh and calf muscles were gone, vanished into the ether of never was.

Losing much of his ability to move, he croaked defiantly.

"I brought her back here and dragged her body into the basement, where I had cleared some room on my old work bench. Then, I put her up there, and we, or I rather, started having sex. Her cunt was still warm. I remember it fondly."

With all of his remaining strength, Walter pushed his coffee off the card table in the kitchen. The cup exploded into innumerable shards—its black insides flowing out and over the crusted tiles.

You sick fuck!

Walter Sr. considered the mess, then he returned his gaze to his dying son.

"A few weeks after I started having regular coitus with your mother, her corpse became pregnant. She was decomposing and stinking, so you can imagine my surprise. Her womb swelled upon her pallid body. And soon enough, a child was born.

"But that newborn baby, your sister, didn't live. She shrieked wildly, with her heart outside her chest, her tiny skull devoid of eyes —and she died, a very malformed fetus. Her bones rest in a mason jar in the basement, beside those of your other siblings."

"Siblings...."

"Yes. You were my seventh child. The only one to live longer than a few months. And you just kept growing and growing, as your poor mother continued to rot in the basement—turning all green and bloated and crisscrossed with purple veins.

"I still went down for occasional sex, but her corpse never bore children again. Soon, there was nothing left of your mother, so I burnt her bones in the furnace and decided to forget the past. To raise you in the present."

"You never raised me, you monster..."

"You are one of a kind, Walter. The perfect marriage of life and death. The embodiment of aging and regenerating in one vessel. Two sides of one coin, made indistinguishable, made flesh... for a few decades.

"As a child, I watched you coldly, wondering how, or when, you would decompose. But you never did. You always defied my expectations... and for that, you were truly better than me."

"I'll kill you... you'll pay..."

"Oh, I suppose I will pay," said Walter's father, shrugging. "In the same way we all do. In the way you are now... with loss of life, with nonexistence. You see, and you should know from experience, that there is not much difference between life and death. You've proven it here, today."

Walter Sr. took a sip of his coffee, regarding his son, who'd further degenerated during his explanation.

Walter was all bones now, with a mere scrap of larynx and lung. His heart beat weakly, and his unsupported skull rolled to its side— his vertebrae stretching, curling.

"The skin, what separates us all from the other side, is just millimeters deep. Not much will change with you in death. I hope that gives you some solace, son."

"*Just millimeters... deep...*" Walter rasped with his final breath.

His heart let out a finishing thud, and he toppled to the floor, a lifeless pile of bones.

THE UPSIDE-DOWN VOICE THAT SPEAKS BACKWARDS

Illustrated by:
Giulio Pappalardo

I READ AND I FLIPPED THROUGH THE PAGES
AND WATCHED AS THE WORDS SOUNDED BY
AND THAT'S WHEN I HEARD THE VOICE
AND THAT'S WHEN I THOUGHT I HAD DIED

IT SAID — "ESOUH YM FO TUO TEG!!"
AND IT SPOKE WITH AN OFF-KILTER SNARE
IT SCREAMED AND IT WHISPERED CONCURRENT
AND ALL I COULD THINK WAS TO STARE

THERE DWELT NO BODY IN MY PRESENCE
NO LIPS FROM WHERE IT HAD COME
SPEAKING UPSIDE-DOWN AND BACKWARDS
IT HISSED WITH ITS ROUGH THROATY DRUM

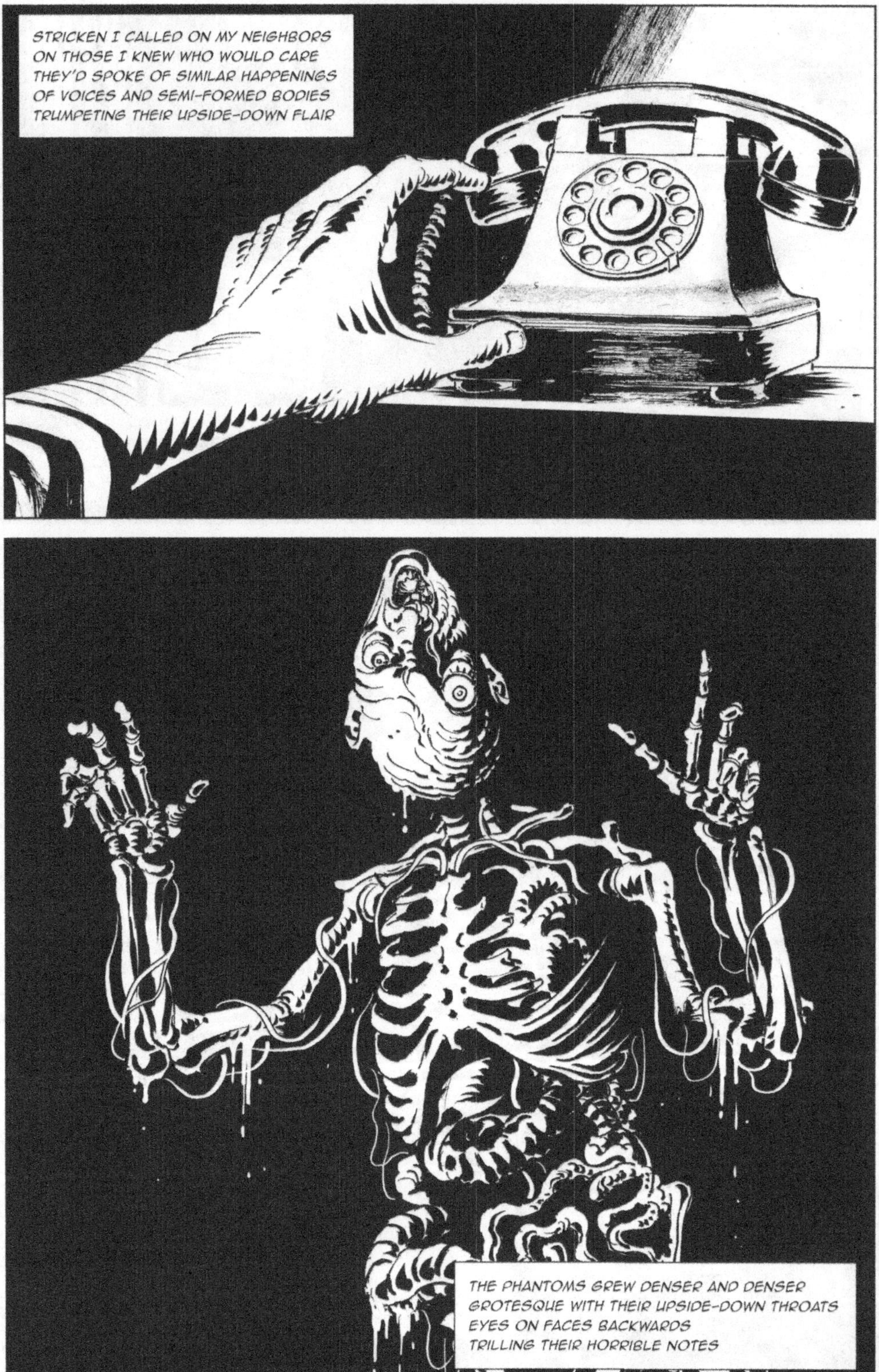

STRICKEN I CALLED ON MY NEIGHBORS
ON THOSE I KNEW WHO WOULD CARE
THEY'D SPOKE OF SIMILAR HAPPENINGS
OF VOICES AND SEMI-FORMED BODIES
TRUMPETING THEIR UPSIDE-DOWN FLAIR

THE PHANTOMS GREW DENSER AND DENSER
GROTESQUE WITH THEIR UPSIDE-DOWN THROATS
EYES ON FACES BACKWARDS
TRILLING THEIR HORRIBLE NOTES

THEIR INVERTED FLESH, MUSCULATURE, AND ENTRAILS RIPPLED, ON THEIR UGLY BODIES CRIPPLED, THEY TWISTED THERE, SLICKED WITH THEIR SICKENING SHEEN

"ESOUH YM FO TUO TEG!!"
WERE THE WORDS REPORTED,
AS THEIR ESOPHAGI WHEEZED AND SNORTED
AS THEIR BODIES WRIGGLED CONTORTED,
SINUOUS, FREAKISH AND GORY AND MEAN

AND THEIR NOSTRILS FLARED UPSIDE-DOWN,
AS THEY MOUTHED THEIR SICKENING SOUNDS
BESIDE BONE STRUCTURES, EXPOSED AND PERVERTED
WHILST LIGAMENTS TENSED AND DIVERTED
AND TERROR MADE ITS HORRIBLE ROUND

US DENIZENS WENT OUT TO THE FIELD, WITH SECRECY AS OUR SHIELD, IN DARKNESS WE PAUSED AND WE KNEELED, PLANNING OUR WAY OF ATTACK

BUT THE CREATURES HAD LAID THERE IN WAITING, AS THEY MUTTERED GROTESQUE AND DEBATING GARBLING THEIR GUTTURAL TACT

"IT'S A MULTIDIMENSIONAL COUP!" MY BIG FRIEND, HE BLURTED, WITH WORDS HE SHOULD'VE SKIRTED FOR HE BROUGHT ON THE VICIOUS ATTACK

THE UPSIDE-DOWNS RUSHED FORWARD, AND DID WHAT WE ALL ABHORRED, 'TWAS MY FRIEND'S SKULL THEY CORED, AS THEY BLUDGEONED AND BEAT HIM...
WITH BATS

SO, I RAN AND I RAN AND I SPRINTED TO MY HOME, WHICH IS OWNED AND NOT RENTED, BUT MY HOPES WERE ALL DISENCHANTED DURING THE FRANTIC, FRIVOLOUS ACT

FOR THE NEIGHBORHOOD LAID UPSIDE DOWN AND BACKWARDS ITS STREETS WERE REVERSED IN INDETERMINATE TRACTS

I SPRINTED AND SPRINTED AND SPRINTED AS TIME TWISTED LABYRINTHINE, BACK CHITTERING ON ITS COGS AND ITS RATCHETS IT SUNG FROM ITS DEVILISH TRACT

PANTING I REACHED MY DOMICILE, RETURNING FROM THE SCREECHING EXILE, TO A PLACE I HAD NOT BEEN FOR A WHILE, I STOOD THERE AND SHRIEKED AND I SCREAMED

AND WEEPING DID COME SOON AFTER, CRUSHED BY THE WHOLE DISASTER, BESEECHING MY EVERY RAFTER, BEMOANING THE SICKENING LAUGHTER—FOR SOME UPSIDE-DOWN VOICE GIBBERED NEARBY

THE OBJECT OF MY DESIRE, WAS TRANSPORTED AND WAS NOW MUCH HIGHER, AND I WATCHED AS MY CHIMNEY CONSPIRED, SIDEWAYS IT BILLOWED AND STEAMED

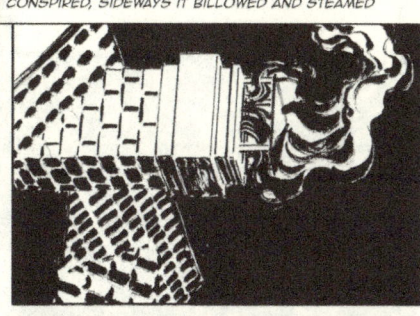

MOCKING ME, A STRANGER, WHO KNELT THERE CRYING AT WHAT I DID SEE FOR I COULD NOT ENTER MY FRONT DOOR FOR UPSIDE-DOWN AND BACKWARDS IT BE.

NO... I COULD NOT ENTER MY FRONT DOOR... NO... NOT ANYMORE... 'TWAS MOVED UP A WHOLE FLOOR

SO, I SCREAMED AND I RAN AND I SPRINTED, AND MY FATE IT WOULD SOON BE HINTED, IN OUR FOREST OF NEWLY MINTED, HORRIBLE EVERGREEN TREES—

THEY WERE UPSIDE-DOWN AND BACKWARDS THEIR BOUGHS GROWING INWARD, DISEASED

I RAN AND I RAN AND HEARD VOICES,
FEELING I'D MADE THE WRONG CHOICES,
HEARING THE SICKO REJOICES

THEY WHISPERED...AND I COULD FEEL...THAT THIS HOME WAS THEIRS,
UPSIDE-DOWN AND BACKWARDS, I'D ENTERED THEIR SERPENTINE LAIR

SOON, THE LAKE RIPPLED BLUE BEFORE ME,
AND MY SIGHT IT DID ABHOR ME, AS I WHIMPERED AND WATCHED
AS ITS DROPLETS ROSE IN THE AIR

AND DROPLETS BECAME
LARGER GLOBULES

AS I STOOD THERE

FRIGHTENED

AND STARED

AND SOON I CALLED OUT IN ALL HORROR,
AS IF I'D GONE THROUGH THE DOOR, OF HADES, OR HELL, OR GEHENNA,
FALLING I FLEW THROUGH THE AIR

FOR I HAD LOST ALL MY FOOTING,
AND THE GROUND
IT WAS NOT EVEN THERE

I PLUMMETED UPSIDE-DOWN AND BACKWARDS
AND DRIFTED THROUGH THIN FOREIGN AIR

I LOOKED

AND I SHRIEKED

AND I PRAYED ALOUD
TO A GOD WHO WAS NOT EVEN THERE

MY VOICE WAS RIGHT-SIDE UP AND FORWARDS
SOUNDING ITS SOLE MORTAL ERROR
IF ONLY IT'D BEEN UPSIDE-DOWN AND BACKWARDS
THEN MAYBE, BETTER I'D FAIRED

I FELL AND I CRIED AND I SCREAMED
"PLEASE HELP ME!"
TO A GOD WHO WAS NOT EVEN THERE

IF ONLY I'D UNDERSTOOD...
THE UPSIDE-DOWN VOICE THAT SPEAKS BACKWARDS
AND THOSE INVERTED EYES
THAT PLOTTED AND STARED

ABOUT THE AUTHOR

R.J. Benetti is a horror author residing in Erie, Pennsylvania. Growing up, he was always drawn to the spooky and the strange, and credits The Twilight Zone, Tales From the Crypt, The Simpsons' Treehouse of Horror episodes, Creepshow, Mars Attacks, Halloween, and The Shining for spurring his imagination and his love of storytelling.

He was recently nominated for the 2023 Splatterpunk Awards for his short story, *Just Another Bloodbath at Camp Woe-Be-Gone* (available on Amazon and Godless). He is also the 2022 Gross Out Contest Scares That Care champion and a Godless 666 Awards Gold Medal recipient.

When he's not writing, he enjoys spending time doodling and watching horror movies with his wife and long-haired chihuahua, named Dwight.

You can find more of his work here:

Godless

Amazon

Made in United States
North Haven, CT
09 June 2024

53434914R00136